Petteril's Baby
Lord Petteril Mysteries,
Mary Lancaster

Petteril's Baby

All Rights Reserved © 2025 by Mary Lancaster
No part of this book may be reproduced or transmitted in any form
or by any means, graphic, electronic, or mechanical, including
photocopying, recording, taping, or by any information storage or retrieval system, without
the written permission of the publisher.

Chapter One

Viscount Petteril, emerging onto the front steps of his London house on a wintry January morning, became aware of a hubbub below.

The disturbance was unusual enough to draw his erratic attention downwards, to where another set of steps led to the tradesmen's entrance. What appeared to be his entire staff, apart from Joshua the first footman who had opened the front door for him, were huddled around something on the lowest step.

At least, he assumed they were his staff. When confronted by a sea of faces, he had great difficulty distinguishing between them. In this case, he recognized the Petteril livery that clothed a young footman and the general shape of his housekeeper, Mrs. Park. And her husband, Park the butler.

There was an air of shock and doom about them. They spoke in the urgent, hushed voices of inveterate gossips, so engrossed that they had not noticed his egress from the house or his approach toward them. They only looked up, all at once, when he set foot on the area steps.

"You look as if you're breaking the combination laws," he remarked flippantly. "What, Park, is to do?"

"You tell me, my lord," Park said with unusual grimness. His underlings fell back, making way for the master of the house.

Intrigued, Piers descended the steps to discover the source of the disturbance. It appeared to be a shallow wooden box containing rags, though what there was in that to cause such consternation was beyond him. He groped for the correct quizzing glass hanging on its black ribbon around his neck and peered more closely.

A tiny patch of creamy pink was visible among the rags, and...it moved.

Startled, Piers dropped his quizzing glass. "What is it?"

"It's a baby, my lord," Mrs. Park said, gazing at him with what looked like disappointment.

Being used to such looks from others, he thought nothing of it. The box of baby concerned him more. "What is it doing here?"

"Sleeping, my lord," said Janey the scullery maid, whom he was teaching to read with some success.

Piers scratched his chin. "Whose is it?"

They all looked at him again.

"We don't know, my lord," Mrs. Park said. "Janey found the mite there when she was putting out the rubbish."

Piers picked up his quizzing glass again, with more than a little unease. "It *did* move, didn't it?"

"Oh, it's alive, sir," Mrs. Park said, much to his relief.

"Then shouldn't you take it indoors to keep it that way?" he asked, in a genuine quest for information. The little creature certainly seemed to be well wrapped up, but he had an idea that infant humans were even more susceptible to cold, damp weather than adult ones. "And you had better inform her ladyship."

Once again, they all looked at him.

"Are you sure you want to do that, my lord?" Park asked cautiously.

Piers blinked. "Of course."

"What if its mother comes by to fetch it?" Francis the footman asked, with the air of one being helpful.

"It's not a bird," Piers said.

"Oh, my lady," came Mrs. Gale the cook's voice from inside the kitchen, flustered to the point of panic. "You'll catch cold out there—I've got the menus over here..."

"What's going on?" asked April, his viscountess, from the open doorway.

Bizarrely, there was a general movement to block her view, but she dealt with that in her usual way, not by the haughty lift of an eyebrow as most ladies might meet such a situation, but by scowling. The sea of servants parted for her, too, though with more reluctance than it had for Piers.

April walked forward and bent over the box. She blinked. "What is it?"

"It's a baby," Piers said.

She looked up at him. "What on earth is it doing here?"

"Sleeping, so I'm told. Though I can't help feeling it should do so inside the house."

"Of course it should," April said, picking up the box and marching inside.

Piers followed her, aware of the servants all exchanging meaningful glances behind him.

April set the box on the kitchen table.

"Mrs. Park!" she exclaimed in sudden fright. "It's moving!"

"Isn't it meant to?" Piers asked.

"Of course it is," Mrs. Park exclaimed, bustling through to stand beside April.

The baby had untangled its head from the covering rags and was breathing quickly and audibly. Its small, pinched face was dominated by a pair of large, intense blue eyes, which seemed to be searching for something. Its lips formed an "O" and the tiniest tongue thrust out between them.

"He's hungry," Mrs. Park said.

April wrinkled her nose. "He smells."

"I'll fetch some milk," Janey said, heading for the larder.

But April was frowning. "Wait, you can't give it cow's milk. It's too small."

"How do you know that?" Piers asked in surprise.

"Oh, I have friends with babies," April said with such studied carelessness that Piers understood. Having babies was an occupational hazard among the prostitutes who had once been casually kind to her. "I don't know any more than that, though. Its mother should feed it. Where *is* its mother?"

"That's what we'd all like to know," Mrs. Park said, glaring at Piers, who blinked in surprise.

"Wet nurse," he said, dredging up his own distant knowledge from somewhere. "Does anyone know a wet nurse?"

"Yes," Mrs. Gale said doubtfully, "but you might not like her."

"Better fetch her anyway," Piers said. "Just in case. Hopefully, the mother will return for it before then. I'm off for my ride."

WHEN PIERS HAD GONE, and Mrs. Park had sent everyone else about their neglected duties, April trailed after her into the housekeeper's sitting room.

Mrs. Park removed the baby from its box and set it on a clean apron on the rug before the fire. As if she knew what she was doing, she unwrapped it from its shawl and its tiny nightgown to reveal the nastily stained napkin pinned around its bottom.

"I've lived too long in luxury," April said, backing off with flaring nostrils.

"Rich babies and poor babies all make the same mess," Mrs. Park said. "Would you send Janey in with a bowl of water and some clean rags?"

For speed, April fetched the water herself, then went upstairs to find a couple of clean shawls. When she returned to the housekeeper's sitting room, the baby was naked and kicking its little legs in a happy kind of way.

"It's a boy," April remarked, unsure of the cause of the pang wriggling through her.

"It is." Mrs. Park whisked a cloth under the child's bottom, pulled it up between his legs and knotted it at either side. Just as if she knew what she was doing. As far as April knew, the Parks had never been blessed with children, yet the housekeeper picked him up and sat holding the baby as if she was his mother.

"What's the matter with his arm?" April said, catching sight of a purplish mark on the otherwise perfect skin of the baby's forearm. "Is it a birth mark?"

"I wondered that, but I think it's a bruise. He must have bumped it on the edge of the box." She regarded April. "He is a little thin, but he has clearly been cared for."

"Until he was abandoned on our doorstep," April said. "You don't just forget your baby like a shopping basket, do you?"

"No," Mrs. Park said. "You don't."

"Unless she was drunk and won't remember until she sobers up."

"Oh hush, my lady, that's not the sort of idea you should be coming up with."

"It happens," April insisted.

"Not around here it doesn't."

That was a fair point. April regarded the baby with a mixture of doubt and awe. Such a tiny, helpless little human...

"My lady, I'd hoped to keep this from you," Mrs. Park said bluntly. "But since you've seen the little mite, you had better consider the possibilities. If the mother was too poor to care for the child, or even if she just wanted better for him, where else would she leave it but at his rich father's door?"

Uncomprehending, April waited for more.

Mrs. Park snatched a breath. "His aristocratic father's door."

April blinked, then let out a peel of genuine laughter. "You think it's his lordship's child? Don't be silly, Mrs. P." The pity in Mrs. Park's face disconcerted her.

"The mite was clearly conceived before you were married," the housekeeper said consolingly.

April frowned at her. But to her own annoyance, she found herself counting. "How old is the baby?"

"A month? Two at a pinch."

"Well, his lordship was in Oxford until…" She trailed off.

"Until March," Mrs. Park said flatly.

April stared at her. "You're wrong. He would never abandon his child, or its mother, with nothing. Besides…" She closed her lips, for in fact, she knew little of her husband's life before March last year. And it was true he had not been at his best when they had first met. "He wouldn't," she finished.

"He might, for your sake."

And damn everything, that might just be true too. On the other hand, she couldn't believe he knew anything about the child, and quite clearly he still didn't associate it with himself.

"Either way, it doesn't hurt me," April said grandly. "And the viscount will always do the right thing."

THE VISCOUNT, IN FACT, was already galloping across Hyde Park before the reason for all those accusing and disappointed stares of his household struck him.

They think the brat is mine.

No wonder they had tried to keep April away from it. He almost laughed, only it stuck in his throat. He did not want his wife imagining such a thing. For himself, he had been so used to the poor opinion of his family that it came as a surprise to realize he had grown used to the approval of his staff as well as his wife.

Slowing his horse, he urged it off the path, turning it back the way he had come, and galloped back toward the gate.

Hoping devoutly that the baby would have been claimed by its mother before he reached home, he walked his horse along Park Lane, then paused at the corner of his own street to buy flowers from the girl who usually had her barrow there.

Her offerings were few in the winter, since they were nearly all expensive hothouse flowers. Ignoring the paler, humbler blooms at the front of the barrow, he bought her remaining red roses with a smile. Bending from the saddle, he collected them from her.

The girl, shivering under her too-thin cloak and hood, whispered, "Thank you kindly, sir," and held up her hand with his change.

"You get off home and stay warm," Piers said severely, and rode on, hoping she had enough money to be warm and fed. Winter was a dangerous season for a great many unfortunate people.

He turned his horse into the mews lane, patting the animal's neck and wishing he rode the Professor, whom he had left at Haybury Court because he had not planned to be in London longer than a few days. Somehow, they had remained here a month, and he was more than ready to go home to the country. Weather permitting. So was April. Next week. She was already packing in a slow, haphazard kind of way.

Abandoning his mount at the stables, he walked through the kitchen garden and entered the house by the back door. Here, he was encouraged by the lack of crying baby sounds, so when he encountered Park in the kitchen, he asked quite cheerfully where her ladyship was to be found.

"I believe Lady Petteril is in her bedchamber, my lord."

Piers was halfway up the steps toward the main part of the house when Mrs. Park emerged from her sitting room with a wriggling bundle in her arms.

Damn it!

He strode on to the entrance hall and up two flights of stairs to April's rooms. He didn't knock, for the simple reason that the line between hers and his had blurred and he spent most of his nights in here. Or she in his room, for variety.

She stood beside the bed, gazing down at an array of what looked like old dresses and bits of bedding, her expression one of rare discontent.

She glared at him. "I can't sew."

"Neither can I." He brightened. "Yes, you can. You made that little satchel for your notebook."

"A square of cloth," she said derisively. "I can't sew a gown for a baby. Can you buy such things? New, I mean."

Piers scratched his chin. "I expect so. You know we can't keep the baby, though. It isn't ours."

"*He* isn't ours," April corrected. She met his gaze. "Is he yours?"

Piers laid the flowers on the bed in front of her. "No."

"Do you *know* that? For certain? He would have been conceived around March last year."

"Around the time you burgled my house," Piers agreed, hoping to make her smile.

She didn't. "Would you remember?" she blurted. "Would you have taken the same care?"

"I didn't need to," he said, quite without arrogance. "By the time I married you I had not been intimate with any woman for over a year. I could give you the precise date and place, but I would really rather not."

She nodded as if that was what she had expected to hear, and yet something in him ached. Lost, somehow, he watched her fingers close around the roses on the bed.

"I brought you these to salve my conscience, of course," he said lightly. "They're less trouble than a baby, particularly when you can make a servant put them in water."

She played the game. "I believe the viscountess can also make a servant put the baby in water." She picked up the roses and to his horror, he saw tears in her eyes.

"April," he said, touching her cheek.

A funny sound, half-laughter, half-groan escaped her as she threw her arms fiercely around his neck. "Of course I know he's not yours. But it's what they all think, and you weren't *paying attention* when I found you."

Piers, who had certainly not been paying attention to women in those black months before April, contented himself with folding his arms around his wife and kissing her soundly. She co-operated with gratifying enthusiasm.

"Ouch," he said as a thorn dug into his neck.

"It serves you right for leaving me alone with a baby."

APRIL, SURPRISED AND slightly ashamed of her emotional reaction to the odd situation, was relieved to have the last vestiges of suspicion removed. Although she would never have blamed Piers for a relationship occurring before they even knew each other, the abandonment of a child had struck too close and unpleasant a chord.

It wasn't that she put her husband on a pedestal, she told herself, as she went down to speak to Mrs. Gale's acquaintance, the wet nurse. She just understood him. It was not so much that he had wobbled, as that *she* had, emotionally speaking.

Oh yes, it was time to go home. She longed for the peace of the countryside, which had once seemed so alien to her. There, she could get her balance back, feel more like herself again.

The wet nurse smelled of gin.

But since the baby was now crying piteously, April saw no solution but to let the nurse feed him.

She drew Mrs. Park aside. "Did you not find the servants through an agency? Would it have wet nurses on the books?"

"I expect so, but is it worth it? If the mother doesn't turn up, we'll have to inform the authorities, give the child over to an orphanage."

"Oh no," April said, appalled. "They are dreadful places." Even she had known better than to go near an orphanage in her darkest hours.

Mrs. Park regarded her uneasily. "You're not thinking of keeping him here?"

"Only until his mother comes back for him."

"And what if she doesn't?" Mrs. Park demanded.

"Then we'll find her. We're good at solving puzzles."

Chapter Two

As it grew dark that afternoon, only her sense of his lordship's dignity kept April away from the kitchen. Instead, she sat in the window seat of the drawing room, from where she could just make out the opening to the area steps.

Surely this was the time the mother would be going home from her work? Or whatever had led her to leave the baby.

Piers came in with his piles of correspondence and sat by the fire. Normally, she liked to watch him at work, admiring the speed and firmness of his hand gliding across the page. Normally, she would read a book, glancing up occasionally. Today, the book lay in her lap unopened, and when she spared a glance from the window, she found he was not reading or writing either. He was looking at her.

"What are you thinking?" she asked.

He stirred. "I'm thinking we've let the tracks fade. We should have begun looking for whoever left the baby the moment we found him."

"We don't know how long he was there *before* we found him," April pointed out. "He could have been there since last night."

"I doubt it. The area is swept and cleaned each morning. Janey would have found him then. Are there not deliveries of milk and butter early in the morning? Besides, he was content and not dangerously cold. I don't think he could have been there very long before he was found."

Like her, Piers had been thinking about it. And for an apparently vague man, he was sharply observant. She had always been fascinated by that contradiction.

"We need to speak to delivery men," April said. "And neighbours and their servants."

"And our own," Piers said.

April frowned. "Our own? But they all assumed the child was yours."

"That's not evidence," Piers observed. "And it's worth pointing out, the baby was not left at the front door, but at the servants' entrance."

"To be less visible from the street, probably," April said. "And if whoever did it was not a lady—or a gentleman—they would be noticed coming up the front steps."

"That is true, but the point remains, why pick on our house? Is there a connection? Or was it just luck that our step was the one?"

"Girls who're in trouble," April said, "mothers who can't cope or who're desperate, leave their babies at church doors or orphanage gates. Who would rely on an unknown nob in Mayfair? Would it not cause scandal and sniggering to take in such a child?"

"Yes," Piers said ruefully. "And believe me, word will spread, if it hasn't already. And whoever left the baby with us must have known it was likely to end up at the orphanage just the same. Which makes me think it was an impulse born of some kind of desperation. A sick or even dying mother."

"Who just happened to be strolling the gracious streets of Mayfair?"

Piers sighed. "What was the infant wearing?"

April wrinkled her nose at the memory. "Something very nasty. A gown of some kind and wrapped in a shawl. With bits of cut-up clothing and other rags as blankets—they were clean." Her gaze strayed back to the window. "The mother could still come back for him."

Piers nodded. "And if she doesn't, we shall begin looking for her in the morning."

"It won't be easy," April said reluctantly. "Not if she wants to stay hidden."

"Oh, I don't know. I found you easily enough, didn't I?"

April smiled at the memory. It seemed so long ago. Another life of fear and nightmare. And yet she was *not* a different person.

"Tomorrow," she said decisively. But she stayed by the window, watching.

AFTER DINNER, THE LORD and lady of the house flustered their staff by appearing in the kitchen for the second time that day.

Mrs. Park, who knew immediately why they were there, ushered them to her sitting room and closed the door. The baby was lying awake in its wooden box, gazing at a candle flame.

There was no sign of the wet nurse smelling of gin, but another young woman, neat in a starched cap and apron, rose as they entered.

"This is Mrs. Robb from the agency," the housekeeper said, and the woman curtsied.

To April's critical senses, she was clean and fragrant, though there was little obvious warmth about her.

"She has agreed to stay on a temporary basis until the matter is resolved," Mrs. Park added.

"Thank you, Mrs. Robb," April said civilly, and to Mrs. Park, "I take it no one has come to claim the child?"

Mrs. Park shook her head.

"Most odd," April said.

Piers had already walked up to a little clothes horse in front of the guarded fire, where a tiny doll-sized gown, a shawl, and some of the other familiar baby coverings—including the once nasty napkin—were hanging to dry. He touched the gown and the shawl, feeling the quality or lack of it.

"Mrs. Park," he said, "how often was anyone out in the area before Janey found the baby in the box?"

"Park unlocked the door first thing as he always does. He likes to step outside for a second, whatever the weather, just to make sure everything is as it should be."

"Presumably it was. And from the door he would easily have seen the infant's box on the step."

"He would. And it wasn't there. It can't have been there either when Janey was scrubbing the steps."

"And what time would that have been?" he asked.

"She must have finished by seven."

"And was that the last time anyone was out there?"

"Yes, I think so..."

"What about deliveries?" April asked. "Doesn't the milk come at seven?"

"Just before. I heard Janey telling the boy off for muddying her step. That was all we had until the butcher's boy came later in the morning."

"So, at some point between seven of the clock, when Janey finished with the step, and—what?—just after nine when she found the baby, someone left it on our steps."

"Apparently so," Mrs. Park said. She was blushing very slightly and April thought it was a sort of apology to Piers for imagining ill of him.

Piers did not seem to notice. "I'll just go and have a word with Janey," he murmured, strolling out of the room as though blissfully unaware of the havoc his presence would cause in the kitchen.

"We want to find the mother," April said.

Mrs. Park sighed but nodded. "What does his lordship want to do with the child while he looks?"

April regarded the baby and the nurse and the housekeeper's once private sanctum. "It's a problem."

"If you wish," Mrs. Robb offered, "I can take him to the orphanage."

April cast her a hostile glance. "Would you take your own child there?"

"My own child is dead," the nurse snapped. "So I do not have the choice."

April felt the blood drain from her face so quickly that she had to hold the back of the chair for support. How could she have been so crass? "I'm sorry," she managed. "That was a stupid and unkind thing to say."

"No," Mrs. Robb muttered. "I spoke out of turn."

More for something else to look at, April went to the baby's makeshift cradle. The child, kicking its little legs, gazed up at her fixedly.

"He can't stay in this room," she said. "Mrs. Robb will have to be with him for tonight at least and the old nursery rooms are too cold. They haven't been aired or cleaned for years..." Decisively, she swung to face Mrs. Robb. "You shall have my dressing room. There is a couch made up there already, with space for the baby's box. I shall merely move a couple of things out of your way."

"But my lady," Mrs. Park said, clearly dismayed. "You will lose your privacy..."

"Oh, I shall impose myself upon my husband," April said grandly. And if that didn't stop the silly suspicions of the baby's paternity, nothing would.

MRS. PARK TOOK A FIRST morning cup of tea to her husband and found him standing just outside the area door, deep in thought. She pushed the cup and saucer into his hands and he grunted by way of thanks.

"It isn't himself," she murmured.

"What isn't?" he asked with rare impatience.

"The baby's father."

"Because he's looking for the mother? That doesn't mean all you think it does."

"He could have put his foot down and sent the child away. That he didn't do so means something. Because he knows the gossip it will cause to both of them."

"To please her."

"Maybe. But he is the sort of man to make suitable arrangements. Not this. It isn't his, my dear. Or hers."

"I know that," he said. "It isn't Simon's either."

She looked at him so long in silence, that he was forced to meet her gaze fiercely, as if he imagined he could thus enforce belief.

"*That* is what we don't know," she said gently. "We must consider the possibility. I will not allow my grandson to be brought up—or die—in an orphanage. And I don't think you would either."

He closed his eyes. They shared the old hurts in silence until he squeezed her hand. "I'll talk to himself. If anyone can find Simon, he can. Though it might lose us our place here."

"He married April," she said. "He does not judge people as others do."

"Nor is he a soft touch. Come, we're letting the cold in."

They stepped back inside and he closed the door.

"PIERS?" APRIL FLUNG out one arm in search of him, just as he slid out of bed.

She snapped open her eyes to discover it was still dark, then remembered they had a plan. She almost groaned for she was still tired.

"Go back to sleep if you like. I'm brave enough to nobble the milkman alone."

"I want to see who else is around," April said, forcing herself to slide out the other side of the bed and groping for the day clothes she had brought through from her dressing room last night. If Piers was appalled by the baby and wet nurse taking over his wife's dressing room, he had given no sign of it.

Nor had they been kept awake by crying, although April had heard a brief wail in the middle of the night. Mrs. Robb was clearly conscientious.

Yawning, April stumbled into her clothes, crammed her hair up anyhow with some pins, stamped her feet into shoes, and wrapped herself in two thick shawls.

The house was stirring, but very quietly. The servants were up. As she crept along the passage to the stairs—without any real reason for creeping—she vividly recalled the first time she had done so. Less than a year ago, convinced she was in an empty house that she was so eager to rob. While Lord Petteril had stood silently swaying on his own balcony...

Her stomach heaved with panic, as it did whenever she thought of that moment. She slid her fingers against his for reassurance and felt the comforting clasp of his hand. And the panic vanished.

They went downstairs hand in hand to discover that the front door had been unbolted. The servants were moving around below, talking. Something clattered and someone laughed, while the lord and lady seized cloaks from the hall stand and escaped like naughty children.

April drew the cloak hood over her hair, for icy rain drizzled through the almost- darkness. The street lamps were still lit, although a familiar figure with his long pole could be seen ambling along the street toward the square, dousing lights as he went. From the trees and the nearby park, birds had begun to sing in a subdued but hopeful kind of way.

For a few moments, the city seemed uniquely quiet and peaceful. Apart from themselves and the lamplighter, no one seemed to be about. Only a few of the grand houses round about were occupied at this time of the year, although by spring, the square would be much busier.

For a little, Piers and April observed from their vantage point by the front door, until the lamplighter approached, whistling softly to himself. Then they walked down the steps toward him.

He touched his wet cap without pausing his tune until April said, "Good morning. Though I suppose it's a bit of a miserable one for such work as yours."

The man stopped whistling. "Oh, it's all the same to me, ma'am. A bit of rain don't hurt me."

"Was it not raining yesterday morning, too?"

"Oh no. Very pleasant morning yesterday. Sharp and cold, like, but dry."

"So it was," Piers said. "You must have passed this way at the same time yesterday morning."

"Yes." The man edged his feet forward, clearly wishing to get on with his work.

"I won't keep you a moment," Piers assured him. "We'd just like to know if you saw anyone out and about when you passed yesterday."

The man looked at him as if he'd grown horns. "Can't say I did. Never do, round here, except someone scrubbing steps sometimes. Or delivering milk. Don't see the milk cart until the park though, as a rule."

"What about a woman with a baby?" April asked.

The man's brow creased. "What woman with a baby?"

"That's what we're asking you," Piers said patiently.

"I ain't seen no woman with a baby. Not ever round here. Sir, Missus."

As he passed on determinedly, Piers and April exchanged glances. The whistling started up again.

"It would be too early anyway," April said. "Janey hasn't scrubbed the steps yet."

A few moments later, they heard the area door open, and amidst a powerful yawn, Janey emerged with her clanking bucket and brush. The lord and lady retreated back up the front steps, but they needn't have worried. Although she began at the top of the area steps, she barely looked up, sweeping and then scrubbing each step and the area below with swift brisk efficiency before vanishing inside. She reappeared briefly to plonk an empty milk churn outside, then closed the door again with a decided snap.

No other servants had appeared to perform the same task elsewhere in the square. But a horse and cart were approaching from the direction of the park, the clopping hooves echoing cheerfully. The cart paused at a couple of houses. A boy leapt down each time with a small milk churn, vanished down area steps and reappeared, presumably with the empty churn from yesterday.

It was a larger churn the boy hauled off when the cart stopped at Petteril House. April and Piers descended once more, veering apart at the foot of the front steps, Piers moving toward the driver of the cart while April went to the area gate to accost the boy, who was already leaping up the steps with his empty churn.

His mouth fell open when he saw April blocking his path and he nearly fell back down the steps.

April smiled. "I believe my maid told you off yesterday for muddying her clean step. I thought I should apologize."

The boy blinked, then grinned and jerked his head downward toward the area. "Oh, she don't worry me none. I get worse. And I've muddied her step again."

April pushed a coin into his hand. "You can't help that. You do a good job." While his eyes were still wide with appreciation at such largesse, she said, "Tell me, did you see a woman with a baby around here yesterday when you were delivering the milk around the square?"

"Never see anyone this time of year, not around here this early in the morning."

"Not even from the other side of the square? Or further along the road perhaps?"

The boy did her the courtesy of thinking about it, but in the end he only shrugged apologetically.

"When you say you never see anyone, you saw my maid, didn't you? Weren't there any other maids telling you off or having a joke with you? Other people passing in the street?"

The boy scratched his head. "Didn't see anyone. Only got one other customer over there..." He pointed across the square. "And I didn't see anyone along that way after."

"What about anyone other than residents?" April asked with fading hope. "Any other carts, carriages, messengers?"

"Didn't notice any," the boy said with a hint of anxiety. He thrust his hand into his pocket as though afraid she would try to take her coin back.

"My thanks," April said. "You've helped me a lot."

The boy looked startled as he leapt back on the cart. Piers had already stepped back beside April, and the horse trotted forward.

"Anything?" Piers murmured.

"No. You?"

"No. But they were a few minutes earlier yesterday. Our mother and child were probably not yet on the scene. I think I'll take a stroll up toward the park on this fine morning."

"Then I'll take a turn about the square. It must wake up soon."

Piers, who had had the foresight to bring a hat, ambled off toward the park. April set off in the opposite direction, but despite the lighter sky, she walked twice around the square without seeing anyone at all.

She was just returning toward the house again when she heard soft, breathless singing drifting over from the far side of the square. A maid had just emerged from the front door of one of the houses there and was using a broom to sweep the step and the short path.

April swerved back across the square. For the first time that morning, she felt uncertain, even nervous. The chances were, the neighbouring servants would recognize her as Lady Petteril and know that their mistresses would not receive her—the viscountess being no better born than the girl sweeping the step.

Worse, if only they knew it.

"Morning, miss," the maid called as she caught sight of April's approach.

Encouraged by the fact the girl had not addressed her as "my lady," or "your ladyship," April said, "Good morning. I wonder if you could help me?"

"I'll certainly try," the girl said willingly.

"I need to find a woman who passed this way around this time yesterday morning. You might have seen her across the square."

"What, at Lord Petteril's house? I believe they are in residence."

"Oh, this woman was not one of the family, or even a servant, though you might have seen her at the tradesmen's door. She may or may not have had a...a bundle with her."

The maid noddled wisely. "Beggar, was she?"

"Actually, I've no idea, but I need to find her because she left something behind, and her ladyship wishes to return it to her."

"That's kind of her ladyship," the girl said doubtfully. "I'd wait for her to come back and get it, meself."

"Oh well, you know..."

"Didn't see anyone though," the maid said in what was becoming a familiar refrain.

"Are your master and mistress in residence?" April asked.

"Not until March, though the rest of the staff will come up next month to do the spring clean for their arrival."

"Are any of the other houses occupied just now?"

"Well, there's Mr. Darcy, the son of the house, two doors down—regular rakehell, he is, so I heard. I don't think his servants need to exert themselves much on his account."

Meaning neither he nor his staff would have been up and about early enough to see whoever left the baby on the Petteril doorstep.

"It's a bit like finding a needle in a haystack," April admitted.

"I can imagine," the girl said sympathetically. "They get silly ideas in their heads, some of the Quality do. Tell, you what, though, miss, you want to talk to their coachman."

April, about to move on, froze. "Lord Petteril's coachman?"

"Yes, the coach was waiting just at their gate... No, wait, come to think of it, it had no crest." She beamed as though in triumph. "In fact, it was a hackney cab, 'cause it had a number."

"A hackney cab stopped at Petteril House?" April said, straightening her shoulders. Really, this was more promising! "Yesterday morning about this time?"

"Must have been," the girl said. "I was doing the step and the brasses—'cause some people—" She jerked her head toward the front door and lowered her voice, "...insist on maintaining appearances, even when the knocker's off the door."

The absence of the knocker was a sign that the householders were not in residence. April was more interested in the cab.

"Did you see who arrived in the hackney?" she asked, trying not to sound too eager.

"Could have been your woman, I suppose, though seems odd to me to travel by hackney and not go to the front door. I didn't see her—carriage blocked my view."

Of course it did.

"*Might* have been a lady," the maid mused. "'Cause the jarvey did get down. Must have been to open the door for someone. Probably wouldn't have bothered for a man."

"I suppose you couldn't see through the carriage window?" April said hopefully. "Or see whether he was dropping someone off or picking someone up?"

"Couldn't really tell." Again, she jerked her head toward her own front door. "His nibs was trying to hurry me up. He'll be doing it again, soon."

"I'd better not cause you any trouble. Thanks for your help. Oh, if you remember anything else, or see anyone odd hanging about the Petterils' house, would you mind just knocking on their door and speaking to Mrs. Park the housekeeper?"

"Right you are, miss," said the maid cheerfully, sweeping a swarm of damp dust and mud into the gutter.

April sneezed.

Chapter Three

Since there was no sign of Piers, April walked around a bit more, spoke to a footman at the opposite corner of the square, and a passing messenger who almost knocked her down in his hurry, without learning anything. By then the square and the streets leading from it were busier. Domestic servants were scurrying about. An elderly lady emerged from a house with a pug on a leash, walking toward the park. Horses and carts passed making deliveries, and costermongers with their barrows were making their early rounds. A few horsemen passed en route, no doubt, for Hyde Park, and a carriage moved briskly eastward.

It seemed to April that the baby must have been left before this time yesterday, for the vast majority of people would surely have reported seeing a baby left on a step. The mother must have done it when no one was around, for she obviously did not want to be caught.

The presence of the hackney seemed the most promising clue so far, though it rather changed the nature of the investigation too. Was it a poor woman in distress who had abandoned the baby? Or someone well off that travelled by hackney?

Was it even a woman?

Mulling it all over, April returned to the house, where Park tutted as he divested her of her wet cloak.

"Best go and change, my lady," he said severely. "Shall I send up one of the maids?"

"Oh no, I can manage. Is his lordship back?"

From the twitch of his brow, Park did not know that his lordship had gone out, but he merely replied, "I don't believe so, my lady. Mrs. Robb, however, is having breakfast in the kitchen, so there is no difficulty in accessing the dressing room. If you don't wake the child."

April grinned. "Oh, I won't!"

She ran upstairs, feeling the chill and damp and rather longing for a hot bath. However, she returned to Piers's rooms, where she had left a few of her things. The fires were lit and warming the place nicely. The washing water was warm, and she was soon much more respectably—and dryly—dressed, with brushed and properly pinned hair.

She wanted to talk to Piers about the hackney, and whatever he had discovered, but since there was no sign of him, and she was sure breakfast would be served any moment, she marched determinedly to the door.

It was then that she heard the baby crying and paused with her fingers on the handle.

The pitch of a small baby's cry had always pierced her. Usually, she had run away from it since there was nothing she could do to stop it. Usually, the baby's mother would feed it. Some would shout at it, or croon at it.

Well, thank God for Mrs. Robb and a house full of servants. She could still run away.

Except the crying kept up, growing louder and more distressed. Mrs. Robb must still be at breakfast and there would be no servants on this floor at this hour, not unless April rang for one.

Which she fully intended to do, just as soon as she made sure the baby hadn't fallen out of his box.

She found herself in her dressing room, where the daybed had been made up again. Beside it, the baby's box sat on a low table and the baby, still inside it, had kicked off all his blankets in a fury. His little face was red, but what broke April's heart were the tears on his tiny cheeks.

Without consciously meaning to, she reached for him and lifted him from the box. The crying broke off in apparent surprise.

"There," April said softly, cuddling him close. "There, no one has abandoned you." *Except your mother.* "And you'll have all the milk you want in just a few minutes."

The baby gazed into her eyes and turned its face into her breast, searching for comfort and sustenance.

"And I cannot help you," she whispered.

She was unlikely ever to have children, because of her past. Knowing that, Piers had married her anyway, loved her anyway. More than anything, she wanted him to have heirs and a family because they would make him happy and he deserved it. This abandoned waif should by rights be Petteril's child, and she wished suddenly it was hers.

He was so warm and vulnerable and helpless, and just holding him comforted him. And her. Emotion pricked, tightening her throat and yet filling her with unique contentment.

"You are a puzzling, magical creature," she informed him, a shade unsteadily, walking with him in her arms and rocking him at the same time. "And your mother must be breaking her heart without you."

A gusty noise escaped him, followed by an expression of satisfaction.

April flared her nostrils. "Though she won't miss *that*. You are also a dirty, smelly creature. A sulphurous spawn of Satan."

The baby gazed up at her adoringly.

AMANDA ROBB WALKED back into the small but luxuriously appointed dressing room she had been given to sleep in and care for the baby—only to find the lady of the house somewhat clumsily changing the child's napkin.

"My lady! You should have rung!" Amanda cried, appalled. "I was only gone a few minutes—"

"Oh, I know. I just happened to hear him crying and then his bottom exploded."

Amanda let out a giggle without meaning to. Not good for the starched, efficient character she wished to portray. "An apt description."

"I don't think it went beyond the napkin this time," Lady Petteril said with an air of pride as she pulled the clean napkin up between the baby's legs. After which, she looked stuck.

"Let me finish it off, my lady. It's why you employed me, after all. And you will wish to wash your hands."

Lady Petteril, who was at least five years younger than Amanda, sat back on her heels, making way for the nurse, who hastily applied the pins, whisked down the nightgown, and settled back against the pillows with the baby. He was snuffling and fussing now because he could smell the milk.

Amanda, who would once never have dreamed of such immodesty before anyone, opened her bodice and began to feed the baby. The little viscountess gazed for a moment, her expression unreadable, before turning with some light excuse and then leaving.

Amanda smiled faintly. She wasn't quite sure about the lady of the house yet, although at least she hadn't tried to dismiss her for taking a quarter hour over her breakfast. The staff were close-lipped and protective of Lady Petteril. And of the viscount, for the most part, although a couple of the younger male staff who had been nudging each other, seemed to imagine his lordship was the child's father and seemed quite proud of him for it.

Fools.

She stroked the baby's head, crooning at him. "There you are, my precious one, mama's here, taking care of you..."

PIERS HAD HEADED TOWARD the park in the hope of encountering early riders who might have noticed a mother with a box full of baby heading in the direction of Petteril House. However, before he even reached Park Lane, he caught sight of the familiar pie seller setting up his stall, which resembled a barrow with a glass box on top to keep his goods warm and dry.

Since he often exchanged a word with the amiable baker, Piers paused to make conversation and bought a pie as an excuse to linger. He was only the first customer, as a couple of Watchmen on their way home, a gardener, a washerwoman, and three working men queued up behind him. It seemed to be too early for the flower seller and the other stall holders who shared this patch.

Piers stood to one side under the doubtful shade of a bare tree, nibbling at the pie and watching the sun rise until the baker was free again.

"You certainly catch the passing trade here," Piers remarked.

"Got my regulars, too. It's a good spot."

"And you'll see the world go by... I don't suppose you saw a woman pass here yesterday about this time or just a little later, and turn down toward the square?"

"Probably saw a few," the pie man said. "But if they don't buy, I don't always remember 'em."

"This one would have had a bundle with her, maybe a box—not large but awkward to carry."

The pie man smiled at an acquaintance waving from the other side of the road. "Never saw anyone like that," he said positively. He turned his head and as their eyes met, Piers had the odd notion that the baker's were not friendly. Even though the man added, "I can ask around if it's important. Reg with the vegetable cart'll be along later."

"And the flower seller," Piers recalled. "Is she not usually here by now?"

"Still trying to get around your missus?" the baker said cheekily. "Nah, Ginny expected to be late today, but I'll ask her and Reg the Veg, if you want."

"Thanks," Piers said, taking another bite of warm pie. "Damn, this is good. No wonder you have regulars. Are you the baker or do you work for someone else?"

"I'm the baker," was the proud reply. "I'll be getting my own shop in a couple of months, but I might keep the stall on too."

Piers, who had seen other customers approaching purposefully, lifted his pie by way of farewell, and sauntered away toward Hyde Park Corner, where he turned left back toward home. He hoped April was having more luck in her inquiries.

Another thought struck him, however, and he returned home via the mews that were another path into the square. The stables and coach houses were hardly busy at this time of year and some were locked up. Coming to his own stable, he gave the rest of his pie to Bernie, the eternally hungry lad who had replaced a certain Ape, and made what he hoped were subtle inquiries.

Of course, there was little point in subtlety since the stable staff would be as aware as the house staff of the baby dumped like an accusation on his doorstep. Nor did he learn anything useful. So, with a sigh, he took himself home for breakfast.

The door to the breakfast parlour was open and he caught sight of April for once before she saw him. She sat at the table, a plate of food in front of her, but both hands hugging her cup of coffee as though for warmth while she gazed straight ahead.

Over the months of knowing her, he had learned to decipher her more enigmatic expressions. By nature, she was sunny and open, and she rarely dwelled upon the difficulties of her past, but just occasionally, he glimpsed them there. If one looked, her eyes were too old for her face. There was a knowledge, a cynicism there, that no one should have cause to possess. She had always had room for understanding and compassion, and she showed it in practical ways, while embracing her new life with him. And she did, despite occasional nerves that amounted to fear of letting him down.

Most worries now, he could read and solve. But the expression she wore now was one he had never seen before. It belonged to that tiny part of herself she kept locked away, even from him. Everyone had one of those, so hers did not trouble him beyond the fact that right now he could not tell if it was sadness. She looked...dreamy.

It lasted a mere instant before she realized his presence and her face lit up instantly. "Piers! What have you discovered?"

"Very little," he said ruefully, going to the sideboard to help himself to some smoked fish and eggs, while she poured him a cup of coffee. "I couldn't find anyone who saw a woman with a baby coming from the direction of the park, though I have recruited an assistant in the pie man at the corner."

"Mr. Newly," April said.

"Is that his name?" Of course she would know. She had run tame around these streets while employed as his tiger.

"Jack Newly. Friendly man but I wouldn't like to be on the wrong side of him."

"I got that impression. But he offered to ask the other sellers in that little patch if they noticed our woman and child."

"Do you think he bullies the flower girl?"

Piers blinked. "I hope not."

"So do I," April said vaguely. "One of the maids at the house directly opposite saw a hackney stopped at our house around the right time."

"A hackney?" Piers repeated in surprise, setting down his plate and sitting beside her. "Janey never noticed that. And we had no visitors."

"Which is what makes me think it could be important. What if the person who left our baby is not penniless and desperate?"

"The nightgown is homemade, cut down and sewn from another," Piers said. "Likewise the bedding and other rags that kept him warm."

"But they had no holes," April pointed out. "And they did keep him warm."

Piers bowed to her greater knowledge there. "It is an interesting line of inquiry," he allowed.

April swallowed her toast. "Also," she said eagerly, "maybe no one saw our woman because there wasn't one. What if it was a man who left the baby? No one would notice a man carrying a box—they would think he was delivering vegetables or just carrying something else if he was better off. The baby was barely visible beneath all those coverings."

Piers groaned. "You are quite right, of course, and have just doubled our already huge pool of suspects. We are now looking for a very, *very* small pin in our huge haystack."

"We need to know who was in that hackney."

"We do. And fortunately, hackney drivers can be traced. It might, however, take a lot of time since we can't know which stand he came from. Unless your maid noticed the number."

"Only that it had one. But one of the other, closer neighbours might have seen."

"The Rentons are in residence, aren't they?"

"I could call on their servants," April said.

Piers regarded her carefully. "Lady Petteril does not call on servants, sadly."

"Well, I doubt Mrs. Renton will be at home to me," April said wryly. "And the maid across the road did not recognize me as Lady Petteril."

"Only because you were huddled in a wet cloak with a hood hiding most of your face. I suggest *we* call on the Rentons. And on that fellow on the other side... Darcy? Strikes me he's likely to have come home from his revels in a hackney at that time of the morning."

"Then why was he dropped off at our door rather than his own?" April argued. "It's not as if his parents are there to scold him for staying out all night."

"No, but he might have been rolling home somewhat disguised and seen the hackney passenger," Piers said. "If he was in any state to recall it, of course. At any rate, I think we should make calls on the residents and question the servants casually on the way out."

"We can try," April said, doubtfully. "This afternoon? That would give us time to call on Aunt Prudence this morning."

Aunt Prudence was his eccentric great aunt, recently home from extensive travels, and recovering from a bout of illness that she regarded as a personal insult. She liked April.

Piers paused, with his hand halfway to his coffee cup. "She has an odd collection of servants."

April only looked baffled for an instant. "Who think we are kind," she said. "Kind enough to look after an inconvenient baby? But by that reasoning, lots of people might have done the same thing. Your Aunt Hortensia's servants. Sir Peter Haggard's. Even Dr. Laine's. Come to that, any of your acquaintances could have tried to palm their offspring off on you."

"I'm not a private orphanage," Piers said mildly. "And none of my friends would do such a thing."

"Your *acquaintances* might. Some of them might even think it funny, or a punishment, since you married me."

"No," Piers said firmly, though her words made him uneasy. "If someone left the baby in the hope of our charity, it must be closer to home."

"Like our own servants," April said with a sigh. "Well, none of our maids have given birth in the last couple of months. Mrs. Park would have noticed!"

"She wouldn't necessarily know anything about the relationships of the male members of staff. Neither, for that matter, would Park."

April speared the last of the fish on her plate. "Well, we are not short of things to investigate. I suppose we should start with the Parks and see what they know."

Piers glanced at his fob watch. "It's almost time for reading class."

Looking back, he had begun to teach reading and writing to those of his household who wished to learn, as much for his own sake as theirs. With his vocation to teach at university shattered by his inheritance of the title, he had hung on to this much more basic teaching as an anchor to his sense of worth. And because he believed everyone should have the basic chance.

A certain Ape had been his best pupil.

Now, as he sauntered off to the library, he thought about young Francis, the under-footman who had been among his first students. Of them all, Francis was the one with the most obvious eye for the female of the species. He was also ambitious—and who could blame him for that?—so in domestic service, he would not wish to marry.

Still, when Francis arrived first in the library with an eager smile and a respectful bow, Piers could not quite imagine him just expecting his master to look after his illegitimate child. Francis must know the orphanage was an option, or the child being sent far away to be brought up on some distant farm. How much did any of them trust their lord and master? How much cause had he given any of them to do so?

Come to that, what would—or should—he do with a servant who played him such a trick?

He would think that one through if and when it became an issue.

He focused, as he always could, on the day's lessons and the progress of his pupils. Though he found himself watching for any signs that any of them were paying him too much attention. Francis and Bernie the stable boy did nudge each other and cast him a quick glance, but that could mean anything.

At the end of the lesson, he made a decision, and instead of sending them immediately back to their duties, he said, "One moment more of your time. I know you are all well aware of the baby left on the area steps yesterday. Did any of you see anything that might help us find out how he got there? Do you know, or suspect, anything about his origins?"

They would not speak in public if they did, but still he hoped to learn from their expressions and reactions. He didn't, beyond the under-the-table kicks between Francis and Bernie who presumably persisted in thinking Piers the father and the devil of a fellow because of it.

Distaste curled in his stomach as they filed out and went back to their normal duties. Mechanically, Piers walked around the large table, collecting books which he shut away in their usual place.

The door opened and he glanced up to find Park hovering.

"My lord. Might I have a word?"

"Of course."

Park closed the door, looking ominous enough to cause Piers a pang of unease.

The man walked a few paces further into the room and took a deep breath. "It's about the baby."

"Then, cough," Piers said cheerfully, before he recognized it as one of his wife's less respectable phrases for *confess* or just *tell me*.

Park did not appear to notice. "There is a possibility that Mrs. Park and I feel you should be made aware of."

"Well?"

"It's unlikely," Park assured him, "but the child might be our grandson."

Piers's eyebrows flew up of their own volition. "I didn't know you had children."

Park shifted his weight to the other foot. "We didn't tell you, my lord. Both because he is a grown man and because we were ashamed."

"Ashamed?" Piers repeated, startled.

Park stared straight ahead. "Of Simon. Our son. You see, he went to prison."

"I'm sorry," Piers said slowly.

"He admitted to assaulting a man and was sent to prison for it. Everyone knew he was our boy and we were dismissed from our last position. Although at least with a character. That's why we came south to London."

Piers had never questioned their reasons. They had always been amiable, efficient, and not without humour. And they ran his household without intruding. Most of all, they had been kind to April.

"If you require our resignations, we will—"

"I don't," Piers interrupted. "But I don't see the connection to the baby."

"The reason for the assault," Park said, "which Simon never gave in court, though it might have earned him a lighter sentence, was a Woman."

The last word was spoken as though with a capital letter.

"She was married to the victim of the assault. Simon, I regret to say, had been…involved with her." Park met his gaze steadily. "To the extent that this child could be his."

Piers frowned. "So you think this baby was left by its mother? Or by her husband?"

"More likely by my son. He wouldn't leave his child with a man who beat his wife. But he couldn't begin to look after it either."

"But your son is in prison."

"Only for six months. He knows we're here. His mother wrote to him though I wouldn't. He is our only child."

There was pain and crushing disappointment in Park that Piers had never guessed at. The apple of his eye, his only son, led astray into tragedy by an adulterous woman… Only nothing was ever as simple as that.

"Where is Simon now?" Piers asked evenly.

"We don't know. No one of our acquaintance has seen him since he was released from prison."

"Would he not come and see you if he was in London?"

"His mother, perhaps. But he knows we are here together."

Piers sank onto the nearest chair. "Yet you think he might have stolen this child from its mother and put it on your doorstep, knowing you would do right by his offspring? And then vanished again?"

"It is an unlikely possibility," Park allowed. "But I cannot rule it out."

"Any more than you could rule me out as the father," Piers said thoughtfully.

A rare hint of colour bloomed along Park's cheekbones. "I regret that it crossed my mind. I don't believe such a thing."

Piers gestured to the chair next to his. "Tell me about Simon. What does he do? Where would he go in London? Does he have any money of his own?"

Chapter Four

When Piers went off to teach his class, April—since it was no longer fitting for her to join in—usually retired to her rooms to practice on her own. Her reading was improving all the time, but she was aware her handwriting would not yet pass muster in Society. It looked like a child's and needed work.

Not that she had many Society correspondents, but it would be good to be able to write to Lady Haggard—Piers's friend's stepmother—and, when they returned to Haybury Court, to Great Aunt Prudence or Piers's cousin Gussie, without shaming Lord Petteril.

Today, however, she was reluctant to go anywhere near her rooms. She, who had always faced up to violent villains and bullies, was frightened of the way the baby made her feel. Besides, she had plenty to find out. So she went down to the kitchen in search of Mrs. Park.

She found the housekeeper in her sitting room, with the door ajar. She was filling in her account book from a pile of receipts, though she looked up quickly as soon as April entered.

April had the notion that she was not the person expected, though Mrs. Park rose at once and invited April to sit in the comfortable chair beside the fire. There was no sign of baby laundry today.

"What do you think of Mrs. Robb?" April asked, feeling her way to the questions she needed to ask about the servants.

"She's sober and gentle and knows what she's doing," Mrs. Park replied. "Though I have to say she's a bit of a mystery."

April raised her brows. "She is? In what way?"

"Not to put too fine a point on it, she's more educated than any wet nurse I ever met, and that includes the respectable ones employed in great houses."

"Perhaps she came down in the world, and if she lost her own baby, this is the only way she can earn a living."

"It must be something like that. Why do you ask? Have you seen something you dislike in her?"

"Oh no."

"It must be a hard job," Mrs. Park said. "Getting fond of a child and being dismissed a few weeks later."

"Is that what happens? Are wet nurses not kept on to care for the children after they're weaned?"

"Sometimes."

April digested that, along with the warning she was sure Mrs. Park was trying to impart. She wished she hadn't given over her dressing room to the child. Why had she? Just to prove she did not blame Piers?

"Mrs. Park," she said determinedly. "Are any of the servants courting?"

Mrs. Park leaned forward. "Francis has a young woman in service he meets on all his half-days. And hers…"

A knock on the door interrupted any further confidences. Martha the maid entered when bidden and dropped a curtsey.

"Begging your ladyship's pardon, but Lady Petteril and Miss Withan have called. They're in the drawing room."

Involuntarily, April glanced at the housekeeper's clock above the fireplace. It was too early for morning calls, which was curious in itself. She rose with an apologetic shrug to Mrs. Park and made her way up to the drawing room.

Since Christmas, there had been a kind of armed truce between herself and the dowager viscountess, Piers's Aunt Hortensia. Although the dowager thoroughly disapproved of April—and of Piers, which was less forgivable—she credited them with finding the doctor who had probably saved her younger daughter's life. As a result, she had let it be known she received the new Lady Petteril to whom she had not been rude for an entire month.

Miss Augusta Withan, known to all as Gussie, was looking better every time April saw her. Which was a testament to both the good sense of Piers's friend Dr. Laine, and the dangerous idiocy of the so-called physician trusted by the Dowager Viscountess. Though still a little thin, pale and drawn, there was now a *hint* of colour about the girl's cheeks and the lively sparkle was almost back in her mischievous eyes.

She even rose, smiling and holding out both hands. "April! How pretty you look. Do forgive us bursting in on you at this—"

"Gussie!" exclaimed her mother. "Ladies do not *burst* nor even mention such a word."

April squeezed Gussie's hands, which still felt a little frail. "Besides, I am convinced your entrance was much more dignified. You're looking well, Gussie." April curtsied to the dowager, whom she should really have greeted first. "Lady Petteril, how are you?"

"I am quite well of course, and so delighted for my girls. Where is Piers?"

"Oh, he shouldn't be long," April said vaguely, for there was no point in setting the dowager off by mentioning the education of servants which she disapproved of. In fact, she probably doubted Piers's ability to teach them, since she persisted in believing his position at Oxford had been some sinecure obtained by his family name.

"We wondered if you had already left town for Haybury Court," the dowager remarked. "When do you go?"

"Next week, all being well."

"I wish you would stay for the Season," Gussie said wistfully. "It would be much more fun."

Not for me, it wouldn't. April kept smiling.

The dowager addressed her daughter. "We shall have to see if you are fit for the Season, Augusta. All those late nights and gadding about..."

"You could always just make a few dramatic appearances," April suggested. "So that when you're not at some party, everyone is looking for you."

Gussie giggled. "I like that idea."

The dowager, who seemed not to have considered the concept of a partial Season, regarded April with clear surprise. No doubt the idea would be her own, soon.

Tea was brought in, though April, still full of coffee from breakfast, had no intention of drinking any. As always, Lady Petteril closely observed her carefully-learned command of the tea tray, but her scrutiny seemed more mechanical than actually looking for fault—a further softening on the dowager's part? Or did she just have something else occupying her mind?

Of course, she's heard about the baby, April thought uneasily. *I hope she isn't reserving her fire for Piers...*

April rose and took the dowager her tea, more to spare Gussie the task than to appear obsequious. Perhaps Piers would stymie her by going out...

Piers, however, wandered in before the second cup of tea was poured, and greeted his aunt and cousin with his usual vague politeness. Accepting his tea from April, he lifted one quizzical eyebrow. She shrugged minutely in response and he leaned his hip against the arm of the sofa she was sharing with Gussie.

"All well, Aunt?" he inquired.

The dowager bridled. "Why wouldn't it be?"

"Because I've never known you to make morning calls at such an hour."

To April's surprise, Lady Petteril made no retort to that. Instead, her face became wreathed in smiles, which was quite startling in its unusualness. "We have such wonderful news we could not wait to impart it. Maria has just been brought to bed of a fine son!"

Maria, Lady Gadsby, was Hortensia's elder daughter who had been married for several years without being blessed by children until now. Although the birth itself was hardly unexpected, it was certainly cause for celebration.

April smiled, glad for the sake of Maria, whom she had only ever seen from a distance, while the exclamations and questions and answers echoed delightedly around the walls. Somewhere, she was puzzled by the odd tightening of her stomach, the surge of feeling she seemed to have no control over but could not recognize. She suspected it was to do with that other baby currently in her dressing room.

She had no reason to say anything about Maria's baby, since everyone else did the talking. So she just kept smiling.

"Of course, we shall be leaving for Barnett Hall this afternoon," the dowager said happily. "Which is why we called so early."

"Both of you?" Piers said, startled. "Is that good for Gussie?"

"Well, I can't leave her behind," Lady Petteril said impatiently. "And right now Maria must be my first concern. If you were a parent, you would understand that."

April's stomach tugged again, in a slightly different way. Piers *should* be a parent. But he had married her. Was love truly enough?

"Why doesn't Gussie come to us?" Piers said.

And of course there was silence.

Because Hortensia will never let her daughter stay under my roof if she can possibly avoid it.

"But less than a week from now you are going to Haybury Court," Lady Petteril pointed out, "which is further."

"Yes, but it is an extra few days for Gussie to gather her strength," Piers said mildly. "We will travel more slowly than you are inclined to today, and we can leave Gussie with you at Barnett Hall on our way. I daresay the country air will do her good."

"I would like to see Maria and meet the baby," Gussie admitted.

There was no point in hiding it. If Gussie stayed, she would tell her mother anyway.

"Actually, we have a baby here, too," April said brazenly. "So you can practice."

Beside her, she felt Piers's body go still, although she knew his expression would not have changed.

"Baby?" Hortensia repeated, staring at April, then blinking rapidly. "Whose baby?"

"We don't know," April said. "He was left on our doorstep. We are looking for his mother."

The dowager's eyes flashed disgust and malevolence, much more in her old style. "It is yours," she hissed. "You are trying to foist your bastard onto our house."

April laughed. Though her stomach had contracted sharply in pain, the accusation was exquisitely funny.

Piers stood so suddenly that her mirth cut off like a tap. The silence was devastating. Both his aunt and his cousin gazed at him with something close to fright. April couldn't make herself look. She wanted to take his hand, but it seemed she couldn't do that either. This was undoubtedly The Viscount, powerful and quite untouchable.

"If that little speech were not so foolish," he said, his voice clipped and freezing in its rare anger, "I would withdraw my offer to shelter your daughter. When exactly does your truly common-place mind imagine that my wife gave birth to this month-old child? Between courses at Christmas dinner, perhaps?"

His words were like lashes, for the dowager and Gussie had been April's guests for Christmas dinner.

Hortensia's face grew red and mottled under his undisguised contempt. Of course, she'd had no way of knowing the age of the baby, but the conclusion she had jumped to said a great deal about her true opinion.

"Don't be coarse," she said hoarsely. She swallowed. "But you are right. It was an entirely foolish thing to say and of course I regret it." Her gaze flickered to April and back to Piers. "I apologize."

"I hope you mean that. I should be loath to cast off members of my own family."

No one in the room doubted he was prepared to do so. The colour fading fast now from the dowager's face showed she understood the warning perfectly. The danger was not yet passed.

Gussie set down her cup and saucer and cleared her throat. "We should go, mama, if we are to finish packing in time. You could take some of my things to Maria's for me, couldn't you? I shan't need so much for a mere few days with Piers and April."

Her assumption that nothing had changed was quite deliberate, though her anxious glance between her mother and Piers proved she was not nearly as certain as she pretended.

Piers strolled over to the bell and pulled it. "Then we shall see you in a couple of hours."

Clearly, he would not honour his aunt by conducting her personally to the door. April wondered if she should do so, in the interests of keeping the peace, but when she rose, the flick of her husband's gaze forbade her. She had never seen him quite like this before. It was really rather...awesome.

"Sorry," Gussie whispered as she quickly embraced April. "It will be fine."

And then Park was bowing them from the room, closing the door behind the visitors who departed rather more subdued than they had arrived.

More timidly than she ever had before, April slipped her hand into her husband's. He was still rigid, although after a moment, his fingers curled around hers.

"When I think about the number of times you have forgiven that old witch—"

"She was sorry," April blurted. "Old habits die hard with her, but I've never seen her capitulate so quickly before." She gave his hand a little tug. "Capitulate is a good word, is it not? I can spell it, too."

His breath caught on what might have been a reluctant laugh. His arm came around her and his forehead touched hers.

"We knew," she murmured. "We always knew what it would be like, and we did it anyway. Nothing has changed, has it?"

He brushed a stray hair off her face, because he knew she was talking about their marriage. "Yes it has. Sometimes, I *like* being the viscount."

Chapter Five

When Piers had told her about the Parks' son—and possible grandchild—they revised their plans. While he would call on the neighbours, April would go alone to Great Aunt Prudence and inquire about her servants while she was there.

"We can pick Gussie's brains about my aunt's servants," he said.

"And Smithy's brain," April said thoughtfully, since the maid would come with Gussie, no doubt for an added layer of respectability.

"Exactly. I'll ask around the hackney stands, and if I've time, see if there's a trace of Simon Park in any of the hostels."

"They'd remember him if he had a baby with him," April said.

"Especially if he came back without it yesterday," Piers agreed.

"Then there's Francis," April said. "Did Park know where his sweetheart is employed?"

"Yes, but we don't want to go barging in and making difficulties for the girl," Piers warned.

"Oh, I won't do that." April grinned. "I'll go incognito. Incognita?"

"Preferably neither."

She nudged him. "Stop being the viscount. We have a puzzle to solve."

Accordingly, they separated, and April walked briskly to Aunt Prudence's house as she had done so often in recent weeks. In the end, she encountered Piers's great aunt returning from a morning walk on the arm of Angus Baird, her general factotum whose position in her household was neither servant nor guest nor master yet bore traces of all three.

April liked him, though he was a quick-tempered, grumpy bear of a man. He was also unfailingly gentle with Aunt Prudence, although he was perfectly capable of scolding her and scowling at her.

In his own way, he was not unattractive, but she doubted he had had time to sow any wild oats in London, even supposing he noticed women other than Prudence.

"Why, it's the little viscountess," Aunt Prudence greeted her, beaming, as they met at the gate of her house—which bore less signs of neglect than it had before Christmas. "Have you come for tea and a gossip?"

"I have, with much to tell you. You're looking well, Aunt Prudence."

"So are you."

In perfect accord, with Baird looking on benignly, they entered the house. Edie the housemaid greeted April with a cheery smile, took everyone's overcoats and hats, and asked if she could bring refreshments.

Impressed by the improvement in the girl's manners, April looked around her and found the chaotic house still clean and bright and cheerful. She nodded approval to Edie who positively grinned.

"Be off with you, girl," Baird growled. "And don't forget the refreshments."

Over rich hot chocolate and cake, April told them about Maria's happy news, and then about the baby left on the Petteril doorstep.

"Good heavens," Aunt Prudence said.

"Odd place to leave a bairn," Baird commented.

"Exactly," April agreed. "We don't know if it was luck, if whoever left it was in a terrible hurry, or if they had some idea that Piers and I would make sure he was brought up safely."

"That's quite a lot of trust," Aunt Prudence remarked.

"People do trust Piers, though."

"And you," Prudence pointed out. "Lots of your acquaintance must know of your improved circumstances."

"Surprisingly few," April said, unoffended by the old lady's remark. Ape had disappeared after all, and only Annie cared. Annie, courtesan and friend from the past had protected her in childhood when she could, and April had recently returned the favour when Annie's lover had been murdered.

Annie had *not* had a baby, and she would never dream of advising anyone to dump their baby on April without asking.

"He was left on the area steps," April told Aunt Prudence and Baird. "Not at the front door. So the connection might be through the servants."

"I think you're wrong," Baird said. "Sounds like an act of desperation to me, not a plan. The baby would be better hidden in the area, that's all. Maybe she went back for it and it had vanished."

"Then why didn't she knock at the area door and ask?" April objected.

"In case she was accused of doing away with the poor wee thing."

This was something April had not thought of either. But for some reason, her own words were distracting her.

"Why didn't she knock at the area door and ask?"

Mrs. Robb had knocked and asked…sort of.

※

AS HE RATHER EXPECTED, Piers learned nothing from Mr. and Mrs. Renton, who lived in one of the houses on the end of the square facing the park. They were very flattered he had called but did not rise early enough to have seen a baby nor even heard a hackney cab before nine o'clock in the morning.

More encouragingly, the footman who showed him out again, said a hackney had driven past, going east when he'd opened the front door around eight or so, but he hadn't paid it any attention.

His insides awash with tea, Piers walked on around the square to the Darcys' home and sent in his card.

A young man he couldn't recall ever seeing before, emerged almost immediately from a door further down the hall.

"Petteril!" he exclaimed, stretching out his hand as he strode to meet him. "Pleasure to see you again!"

These were the kinds of moments Piers never got used to. He had no idea he had even met Darcy before, but apparently he had.

If this was, in fact, young Mr. Darcy. Which he didn't know either. Therefore, he smiled and shook hands cordially without speaking, hoping the gentleman would give him a hint.

"Care to come through? I'm sorting my snuff."

Somewhat baffled, Piers followed him back to the room he'd emerged from, which was lined with shelves full of jars, all labelled. A glass cabinet displayed a rather beautiful collection of snuff boxes. No one else was in the room, which smelled strongly of spice and tobacco, so Piers gathered this was indeed young Mr. Darcy.

"Bit of a hobby of mine," Darcy said. "Got to do something other than drink and dance and play cards, eh? Got a preference, yourself?"

"About snuff?" Piers said cautiously. "Don't care for it to be honest. Knew a fellow at Oxford whose clothes were positively covered in the stuff—put me off, rather."

"Sounds like a dashed waste," Darcy remarked, shaking a concoction he had clearly just mixed into the small, enamelled box beside him.

"Pretty box," Piers remarked. "I'm afraid I've come on a slightly different errand. You may or may not have heard that someone left a baby on our doorstep yesterday morning."

Darcy paused in the act of taking a pinch of snuff, his fingers halfway to his nose. "Baby?" he repeated.

"Baby. About a month or six weeks old, I'm told, and we can't find a trace of its mother."

"Gone to ground, dear boy, and left you holding the baby." Darcy placed the snuff on the back of his hand which he tilted toward each nostril in turn and sniffed delicately. "Which I suppose makes a change."

"The child isn't mine," Piers said mildly. "But I need to know where he came from before we decide what to do with him. I don't suppose you were up and about between seven and eight of the clock yesterday morning? Or even a little later?"

"No idea, to be honest. I rolled in with the dawn. I think. Not entirely sober. Snored all day."

Piers persevered. "How did you get home? By hackney?"

"No, I don't think..." He scowled. "No, I walked, for a damned hackney nearly ran me down in the square! I'll swear the horses tickled my ears and the carriage tore a hole in my coat."

"You mean you were actually knocked down?" Piers demanded.

Darcy considered. "Might have fallen down. Been a long night, y'know. Gave me a fright, though, and I had to pick myself up. Again."

"But you've no idea what time this was? Was it light?"

Darcy set down his snuff box and scratched his head. "Getting there," he said at last.

"Excellent," Piers said encouragingly. "That's very helpful. Did you see if there was anyone inside the hackney?"

Darcy did think about it, quite eager to please. "I couldn't tell," he said at last.

"Did you see a number? Or could you describe the driver? Or the horses?"

"They were all dark and he wore a hat."

Piers waited optimistically for more, but that appeared to be all Darcy had. "Well, if you think of anything else, pop across the square and let me know. Or my wife."

"Happy to, old boy. Tell you what, Petteril, are you engaged for the evening? Dashed dull in Town just now for the most part, but a few bang-up fellows have got together a bit of a party tonight at White's, if you'd care to join us?"

"That's very kind of you," Piers said, oddly touched. "If I'm passing White's, I'll most definitely drop in."

He wouldn't, of course, since his chances of actually locating Darcy among the sea of faces at White's were minimal. As always, he tried to focus on something other than his companion's face—the colour of his hair, the length of his side whiskers, the sound of his voice—but he was fairly sure he would walk right past him anywhere but in the man's own house.

Still, Piers took his leave with great affability and went in search of hostels and hackneys.

JAMES DARCY GAZED AT the door of his snuff room for some time after his distinguished guest had left. The world knew Lord Petteril for an eccentric—Darcy rather liked that about him—but he was also rumoured to be dashed clever behind his quizzing glasses and amiable vagueness. Darcy rather thought that the haughtiness some of the younger men complained of was due to his mind being on other things beyond their ken. Or just to shyness.

Darcy understood shyness. He was rather shy himself, which was why he drank so much. The alcohol loosened his tongue and his self-consciousness and enabled him to have more fun.

A lot more fun.

Absently, he took another pinch of snuff—it must have been too much for he sneezed violently. He pushed the box away from him in annoyance. Petteril's questions annoyed him too. Or perhaps *worried* him was more accurate. It wasn't that he had begun to forget things—though he was aware that too much blue ruin and brandy could do that to a man.

He sat down, rubbing his forehead. Truth be told, he had given himself a fright and had been on the wagon last night, for he really had not cared for the odd flashes of memory from the night before last.

And he was very afraid those memories involved a baby.

He had certainly dreamed of a baby, for in a hazy kind of way, he recalled giggling over one in a box, and it might just have been on Lord Petteril's area steps, though he couldn't think what the devil he could have been doing there.

Must have been a dream, he told himself. *I certainly didn't put an infant there!*

Or did he? The girl who shared Lucious Lila's rooms had a baby.

Please, God, tell me I didn't filch that baby and leave it on Petteril's doorstep...

"Of course I didn't," he said aloud. "Even drunk as an emperor I'd never have touched a damned child."

It was just a fragment of a dream. It didn't seem to have any connection to the flash of horses and hackney cab which had caused him to fall down in the square. The hackney seemed to be real, so the unrelated baby image must be a dream. That was logical, wasn't it?

He scratched his armpit, and thought he could probably do with a bath before he went out this evening. In fact, he could do worse than go out early and just drop in on Lila to be sure the brat was still there. If it wasn't...well, he would have to do *something* to make things right for himself.

AS SHE WENT IN SEARCH of a hackney rather than go home and order the carriage, April found herself wistful for the days when she could just leap onto the backs of vehicles going in the direction she wanted and jump off again when they veered from her chosen course. She amused herself with the vision of young Lady Petteril hurling herself onto the footman's plate at the back of a town conveyance and carriage-hopping her way to the agency, skirts billowing in the breeze...

In the end, of course, she travelled inside the hackney, like the lady she now was, and caused quite a flurry as she stepped into the agency favoured by Mr. and Mrs. Park. Though she always assumed such places would know her for a fraud and was prepared to fight with all the weapons she had to get the information she needed, she need not have worried.

The agency staff fell over themselves to please her, until the manager himself invited her into the privacy of his office. If he was disappointed that she refused tea, or that she had not come in search of more staff, he did not show it but kept smiling.

"My errand concerns Mrs. Robb," she said, "whom you sent to us yesterday as a wet nurse."

"I trust she is giving satisfaction?" the man said, a first hint of anxiety in his fading smile.

"The baby does not complain," April assured him. "But as you know she was engaged on a purely temporary capacity. If we were to employ her in the longer term, we would like to know more about her. Of course, I am aware from Mrs. Park, my housekeeper, that the woman had character references. But how well do *you* know her?"

"I have to say it was a pleasure to encounter a female of such class looking for such a menial position, and of course, any new mama would be bound to want the best for her child—"

"Indeed," interrupted April, who could spot someone avoiding the question within three words. "So, Mrs. Robb has been registered with your agency for some time?"

He shifted in his seat, taking off his spectacles and polishing them with a mercifully clean handkerchief from his pocket.

"In fact," he said hastily when April raised her brows threateningly, "she registered with us only yesterday, a mere few hours before your Mrs. Park called on us. Of course, we thought at once of Mrs. Robb—such a rare discovery—for the position."

"Indeed..." Were her suspicions justified? Had Mrs. Robb, for financial or other reasons, abandoned her baby on the Petteril's doorstep with the intention of then looking after her own child at their expense?

If so, then she had lied to April's face about her child's death and, presumably, to Mrs. Park and the agency. "Do you know when her own baby died?"

"She did not say, only that it was recent..."

"Might I see what information you have?" Such as Mrs. Robb's address, if she had one.

Half an hour later, she came to a halt outside a respectable house—one of a row of similar houses, built in the last ten years or so. What on earth was she going to find here? Why would a woman who lived in this relative prosperity abandon her child and then seek him out again? Even if her story was true, why would she be seeking such menial work?

There was only one way to find out. April walked up the path and rapped the knocker. A maid opened the door and bobbed a curtsey.

April presented her card. "Mrs. Robb, if you please," she said, in imitation of Aunt Hortensia in one of her pleasanter moods.

"Who?" the maid said blankly, blinking at the card before her eyes widened and she curtseyed again. "Ma'am," she added hastily, "that is, my lady!"

"Mrs. Robb does live here?"

"Oh! No, ma—my lady. Mrs. Robb's the *previous* tenant who just moved out. Poor widow, she was, couldn't stay here once her husband died."

"Then where did she go?"

"I don't know ma'am. She left everything but a few clothes in a bag. And the baby, of course."

So there *was* a baby!

"Then you saw her leave? What did she carry the baby in?"

At this point, April was sure the maid would have closed the door in her face, had the card inscribed *Lady Petteril* not been clutched in her hand. There were definite advantages to being the viscountess.

"What was it carried in?" the girl repeated uncertainly.

"In a cradle? A box?"

"Oh no, ma'am. She just carried it in her arms."

"Was this yesterday?" April asked. "The day before?"

"Oh, no, my lady," the girl said in some relief. "Must have been a fortnight and more ago."

Then where did she go? "Would you mind inquiring of your mistress if she has a forwarding address for Mrs. Robb?"

The mistress of the house, however, almost more flustered than the maid, could not help on this score. Mrs. Robb had been evicted by the landlord for not paying her rent and had, presumably, vanished with her child, into the faceless sea of London's poor.

ON HIS WAY TO THE HACKNEY stand in Oxford Street, Piers detoured to two men's hostels and an inn. None of them claimed to have heard of Simon Park, although of course he might have been using a different name. In each case he suggested Mr. Park might have had a small baby with him. One hostel told him they didn't allow children. The caretaker of the other just stared at him. At the Golden Cross Inn at Charing Cross, he was told he'd never see a man with a small baby because they were women's business.

Hoping for more help from hackney drivers, Piers moved on to the nearest stand at Westminster. Right next to the seat of parliamentary power and privilege lurked the swamp of poverty, crime, and vice known as the Devil's Acre, to which he had been introduced at Christmas.

It crossed his mind to wonder if one of April's family had sent a struggling mother and child to their doorstep. But he would talk to April before venturing there.

At the hackney stands, he received several glances of disbelief. "How am I supposed to remember every passenger I have in a day?"

one driver demanded. He had a particularly large wart on the side of his weathered red nose.

"Well, you might, because this was very early yesterday morning and there was a baby in a wooden box, *possibly* carried by a desperate young woman, but definitely going to Hyde Square in Mayfair."

"Well, that's where you're wrong," the Westminster driver said triumphantly, "because I didn't start until midday yesterday. Never do."

Piers touched his hat and tried the next driver in line. This fellow scratched his head beneath his somewhat disreputable hat. "Not much call for hackneys here so early in the morning. More likely to pick up *in* Mayfair."

"Did you?" Piers asked, hopefully. "Yesterday?"

"Nah."

It was slow and spirit-sapping work, so by the time he got to Oxford Street, he was prepared for further disappointment. At least the stand was bustling, though brisk business meant he had little time to ask his questions, before the jarveys brushed him off in favour of actual passengers.

So he wandered up to a group of drivers whose vehicles were a few yards away from the actual stance while their horses rested.

"Excuse me for interrupting, gentlemen," Piers said amiably. "I'm trying to trace a small child who was abandoned and I have reason to believe a hackney driver may have witnessed—or even carried—the passenger who left him."

"Bless my soul," said one, clearly shocked. He even took off his hat to reveal an entirely bald pate, as though in respect for the dead.

"Oh, the babe still lives," Piers hastened to assure them. "But obviously we need to know to whom it belongs. I don't suppose any of you were working at dawn yesterday?"

A couple of them, including the bald man, nodded.

The other wore a bright red muffler against the cold. When his head moved, the muffler shifted down from his nose to his chin. "Didn't have no baby in me cab, though," he said nervously.

"The baby," Piers said, "might not have been visible. It was probably in a wooden box and resembled a pile of rags more than a living being. Your passenger might have been a poor, desperate young woman..."

"How'd she afford the fare, then?" asked the bald man.

"That is what has me stumped." One of the many things that stumped Piers right now. "At any rate, there seems to have been a hackney in Hyde Square around seven or eight o'clock yesterday morning."

"Not me," said the muffled man with clear relief. "No one goes to the park that time of the morning."

"True," said the bald man. "Certainly wasn't me. Didn't even see any babes in arms—or boxes—that morning. Or any other. Tucker here's the one who's always lucky with families."

"Fill the whole cab up, and dirty it too with sticky fingers and snot," the third man said, speaking for the first time. He was younger than the other two, and wore a white Christmas rose in his threadbare buttonhole. "Not yesterday, though. Don't normally start so early. Day before, I had two whole families. Nowhere near Hyde Square. 'Scuse me." He moved away to his horse who was restlessly pawing the ground and showing signs of taking himself for a walk.

It was certainly too cold for the horses to be still for too long, so Piers didn't blame him. What troubled him was his sense that the man was lying.

"What's *his* name again?" Piers asked the others as the third jarvey walked his horse into the traffic and along the road past the stand. "Just so I can cross you all off the list of drivers I've spoken to."

"He's Amos Tucker. I'm Brearly and that's Smith," said the bald man, flexing his arms and nodding. "Good luck to you, and the poor little mite."

Piers thanked them and walked away in the same direction as Tucker. It had struck him that the younger man looked just a little more refined than the others. And that he was around the right age to be Simon Park. Although he had been trained as a gardener, not a coachman, Simon was apparently good with horses.

But when Piers reached the first corner, the traffic had swallowed up man, horse and cab. Still, he knew now where to find him.

Only how the devil was he to recognize the man, let alone describe the man to Park? In Piers's head, Tucker's features were already the same as everyone else's.

Chapter Six

April's pity for Mrs. Robb drowned any sense of triumph in her discovery of the woman's origins and behaviour. How much harder than being born into a wretched life was being thrust into it from relative prosperity? Mrs. Robb would not have been rich, but she would always have had *enough*. Until her husband died young and left her with nothing but a new baby to care for. With neither experience of work nor someone to care for her child, how was she to earn money?

In such circumstances, April understood being lied to. She needed to consult with Piers, and confront Mrs. Robb—in that order, for they had to think what was best for the baby and his mother.

She should have turned for home immediately, yet on impulse, she walked up to the front door of the house next door to Mrs. Robb's old residence. The lady of this house remembered her old neighbour well, thought it terribly sad, but had no idea where poor Mrs. Robb had gone. Neither did the lady on the other side.

It was on the fourth house she tried that she finally found someone worried about the evicted widow. A young woman called Mrs. Carter had been Amanda Robb's friend and missed her terribly.

"Do you know where she went when she left her old home?" April asked.

"Of course I do. I've been to see her often, only she stopped writing and I haven't found the time..." Mrs. Carter lowered her eyes.

"Could you give me her direction?"

Mrs. Carter glanced up again with determination. "I'll do better than that. I'll take you."

This, April felt, was best of all.

As she had presumed, Mrs. Robb had not moved to a salubrious area, but to a room in a tenement building near Whitechapel.

"I know," Mrs. Carter said ruefully, though April had said nothing. "But the neighbours are mostly decent, and she's got the whole room to herself."

April, who would once have sold her soul for such a privilege—or even for the roof—appreciated the point. How would she feel now, going from Petteril House and Haybury Court and Sillitrees, to such a room? Not so long ago, it had been the height of her ambitions.

As Mrs. Carter raised her hand to knock on the door, a baby cried, surely somewhere else in the bowels of the building? The door opened, increasing the volume of the crying, and a middle-aged woman with white hair regarded them in surprise.

"Yes?"

April's gaze darted beyond her. There was a child's cot in the far corner and the blankets were being kicked around by unseen little legs. What on earth...?

"Oh," Mrs. Carter said. "I was looking for Mrs. Robb. Does she not live here anymore?"

The baby gave a particularly imperious wail.

"Of course she does," the woman said. "I'm just minding my grandchild. Excuse me."

The woman spoke well and politely, like Mrs. Robb herself. April was totally confused as she watched her march across the room to the cot and pick up the kicking, squalling baby.

"This is Esther, Amanda's daughter," Mrs. Carter said to April, smiling with relief.

The baby smiled back, for not only was it a girl, it must have been at least six months old.

APRIL TOOK A HACKNEY as far as the sellers' stalls at the corner of the square, for she had just recalled that Gussie would be gracing them with her company this afternoon and she should brighten up the best spare bedchamber with some flowers.

Before she confronted Mrs. Robb in private.

At first, she thought the flower-seller had gone, then she glimpsed her with only a few hot house flowers drooping in her barrow, half-hidden behind Jack Newly the pie man who greeted April with a smile.

The flower girl smiled too, shivering in her hood. "Sorry, ma'am, don't have much," she said apologetically. "The hot house flowers cost so much, and I can't get the variety."

"They'll perk up indoors," April said optimistically. "I'll take them all, since I have visitors."

The girl's eyes widened as if she couldn't quite believe her luck, and with a little grunt of excitement, gathered them all together. April paid, with thanks and turned away, because the girl made her feel uncomfortable in her new privilege.

Her arms full of flowers, she still managed to drop a coin into the baker's apron. "Have one of your own excellent pies," she murmured. "Did any of your fellow stall-holders see anything of the baby my husband asked you about?"

"Sadly not, ma'am," Jack Newly said, looking her in the eye. "I asked some of my regulars, too, but no one saw anything. Suppose no one's very awake at that time of the day."

April sighed. "Thank you for your help."

Piers had not yet returned, but she barely had time to inspect Gussie's room, arrange her flowers and place another coal on her fire, before she heard the unmistakable sounds of arrival.

"I timed it well, did I not?" Gussie greeted her. "Just in time for tea."

As soon as they were alone in the drawing room, Gussie said in a rush, "Sorry about Mama. Anyone else jumping to the wrong conclusion would have blamed Piers."

"They already do, I'm sure."

"Mama has never been able to see his attraction. Or she pretends she can't. It's grief, you know, because Piers survived and my brothers didn't."

"Neither did Piers's brother," April pointed out.

"She's not good at considering other people. She only knows how to love her own children. But believe it or not, there are signs of progress. If you care, and you really don't need to. To better gossip—how is the baby from your doorstep? Have you found it a home? Or a mother?"

April sighed. "No. Not yet."

Piers did not come home for tea. Although Gussie chattered away in her usual style, April could see she was flagging and took her up to her room for a lie down, leaving a scattering of novels for her.

"How pretty everywhere is since you married Piers," she said sleepily.

April left her to it. She wouldn't have minded a lie down herself.

At the top of the stairs, she paused, looking toward her own rooms, wondering whether to speak to Mrs. Robb now. She certainly had much to say, and to ask, and she was conscious of quite a powerful urge to see the baby. It was not an urge she should give into. The baby was not hers any more than it was Mrs. Robb's, though at least the other woman could feed him and look after him.

The choice was taken out of her hands when she heard a familiar voice in the hall below. It belonged to Dr. Gilbert Laine, an old friend of Piers's, who had stopped the constant bleeding of Gussie and encouraged a regime of healthy food, rest, and fresh air. April liked him and so hurried downstairs to greet him at the drawing room door.

"Come in," she said warmly, signalling the maid for fresh tea. "Though Piers is not home yet, I'm afraid. Or have you come to see Gussie?"

"Miss Withan?" He looked surprised. "No, I didn't know she was here. I am not due to see her again until Friday."

"Ah, Lady Petteril left in a bit of a rush and must have forgotten to inform you. She has gone to her other daughter in the country to greet her first grandchild, and Gussie has come to us for a few days. Though we did want to ask you if she would be fit to travel next week..."

Over tea, Dr. Laine told her that he and his betrothed had set a date for their wedding, and he'd called to ask Piers to stand up in church with him. And of course, he hoped Lady Petteril would attend the wedding breakfast.

April met his gaze. "Are you sure?" she asked bluntly.

"Quite sure."

"Then I would love to," she said, touched.

Dr. Laine finished his tea and set the cup in its saucer. "I shall have to catch Piers another time, I think. But you will pass on the message?"

"I will." She took a deep breath and appalled herself by making a decision. "Dr. Laine?"

About to rise, he paused, his hands resting on the arms of his chair. "Yes?"

"Might I...consult you? Professionally, I mean. Privately." Meaning she did not want Piers to know. She cringed inside.

"Of course," he said, his eyes widening. "Do you mean now? Or would you like to come to my consulting rooms in—"

"Oh, no, I would lose courage long before I got there. It had better be now."

He leaned back in his chair again, his hands loose in his lap. "Then please, tell me how I can help."

April twisted the fine muslin of her gown between her rigid fingers and forced herself to let the fabric go. "Piers and I have been married since the summer, and I know he wants an heir."

"That is not so long," he said reassuringly.

And in fact it was less long if one considered that it had been September before there had been any chance of her conceiving. But anxiety over the length of the time was only an excuse to ask the question she needed answered.

"I'm afraid my body was damaged," she blurted, "in a childhood accident. Is it still possible for me to bear children?"

A frown of concern flickered across his face. "May I know the nature of the accident? Which parts of your body were affected?"

Her hand strayed to her hips and she gestured lower. "I don't recall. I think there was damage...inside." *God, why did I begin this? Can I just walk out?*

"Have your monthly courses always been normal? Regular?"

"Oh, yes."

He nodded. "And about the accident, do you suffer pain still from what happened?"

April shook her head.

"The human body can heal itself quite efficiently, though of course I can give you no certainties."

She nodded, wiping her palms against the sides of her gown.

"Would you like me to examine you?" he asked gently.

She jumped to her feet. "God, no! That is, no thank you, I don't believe that is necessary at this stage. As you say, it has only been a few months, and you have quite reassured me. I am so sorry to have kept you."

As though he quite understood her excruciating embarrassment—he didn't—he rose to his feet.

"Come and see me whenever you wish," he said, following her to the drawing room door. "And there are specialists I could recommend. But my best advice is not to worry about it. Enjoy what you have."

For no reason, she wanted to cry. "Thank you," she managed. "You are very kind."

She showed him out herself, since there were no servants immediately visible, then closed the front door and leaned against it, her heart thundering, waiting until she heard the horses at the door trotting off.

Well, she had asked. Sort of. Without giving him any information to work with, which meant she could hardly be satisfied with his answer. But she knew for herself, didn't she? She had always known.

She wiped her sleeve across her eyes, in a gesture that inspired both guilt and laughter, and a very loud sniff, just as the door heaved at her back.

Jumping forward, she opened it wide and beheld her surprised husband on the step.

"Piers," she said in pleased surprise.

"April," he returned gravely, removing his key from the latch. "May I come in?"

She almost pulled him inside, thrusting the last half-hour to the back of her mind. "I have so much to tell you. Let's go to the library. Oh, you just missed Dr. Laine. He wants you to be the groomsman at his wedding."

"Yes, he told me as he galloped off. I shall have to start composing my speech. Is Gussie here?"

"Lying down in the spare room." Opening the library door, she led him inside and almost pushed him into his favourite chair, then quickly fetched him a small glass of brandy which she presented while kneeling at his feet. She needed to make things normal again, and this was the best way she knew. Sitting at his feet in the library, talking about puzzles and life and small things that were exquisitely funny.

PETTERIL'S BABY

He kept his gaze on hers as he drank from the glass, then passed it to her. She took a sip, then passed it back, and lowered her bottom onto the floor. She laid her head on his thigh and sighed.

This is better. This is how we are meant to be.

For a few moments, she just absorbed his presence, his warmth, the gentleness of his fingers idly caressing her hair. Then she said, "Mrs. Robb's baby is not dead. She lied to us. I thought our baby was hers at first, but it isn't. Her baby is more than six months old. And a girl."

"Cor," Piers commented, and she giggled because it had once been her favourite expression of surprise and appreciation. "I might have found Simon Park—entirely by accident, you understand—but naturally I can't tell."

SOMETHING ABOUT THIS latest puzzle in their lives was bothering April. Piers was aware of it, even as he sensed her settling back into the comfort there had always been between them. He liked that she still needed him in this way. In truth, the unconditional belief of this vital, fragile yet strong little creature, male or female, servant or wife, had always been balm to his weary soul.

Her trouble concerned him, but clearly she was not ready to talk about it. She might not even know what it was herself, for she was eager to talk over the mystery of the baby, and how the various bits and pieces they had learned fitted together. Or didn't.

"So, we know there was a hackney at our house at about the time the baby must have been left," she said, "since the maid across the road saw it, and Mr. Darcy was almost run over by it. And the Rentons' footman thinks he might have seen one. Why was it in such a hurry to dash off after idling at our door?"

"Because whoever left the baby was bolting before they could be seen?"

"Simon Park being not the passenger but the driver of the hackney?"

"It's a possibility, but an odd one. If Simon abducted his newly born child and travelled south with him, how did he feed him on the journey? *And* while he began his career as a hackney driver. The other jarveys had clearly known him at least a few days." In fact, in telling the story to her, he realized the thinness of his theory.

"I suppose there could be any number of reasons he didn't like answering questions," April mused. "He could have been involved in some other nefarious business, totally unrelated to our baby. Or he may have some tragedy in his life that made talk of babies difficult for him."

Piers sighed. "Or he just couldn't be bothered with strangers asking what seemed like stupid questions to a man who needed to earn an honest crust."

"What about Mr. Darcy? Was he telling the truth?"

Piers sipped his brandy, then brushed the glass against the back of April's hand where it lay on his knee. She lifted her head and accepted the glass.

"I don't know," he admitted. "He didn't look remotely embarrassed to see me, made no effort to shake me off. He even invited me to a no doubt riotous and financially ruinous party at White's. But I could swear he was keeping something back."

"Maybe he was just embarrassed that he couldn't really remember anything except falling over in the street."

"Maybe." Piers took the proffered glass back from her. "Incidentally, where have I met him before?"

"He was at the theatre just before Christmas and waved to you. So you must have met him before that - last spring, probably at Lady Petteril's ball."

"Perhaps," Piers allowed. He was sure he didn't know the man well. He drained the brandy glass. "I could almost imagine him being so bosky that he found it amusing to pinch some poor child and dump it on the doorstep of the highest ranking aristocrat in the square, just for a prank. But surely even the most irresponsible of rakes would not do such a thing with his own son?"

"I don't see that it's any better—worse, in fact—to do it to someone else's." April, resting her chin on her interlocked hands on his knee, was scowling blackly.

"Oh, you are right, of course. I'm just trying to understand him and no doubt maligning him in the process. Anything untoward in Aunt Prudence's house?"

"I don't think so. I went down to the kitchen before I left, and all the servants seemed genuinely surprised and outraged by the abandonment of our baby. We did investigate them pretty thoroughly before Christmas and I really can't see them behaving as they do and encouraging someone else to dump their child on us." She sighed. "We're not really much further forward, are we?"

"We may never be," Piers warned. "It was always like looking for the proverbial needle. But I don't feel we should give up just yet. We have, after all, stirred up a few pots. We need to keep our eyes on them while making further inquiries."

They talked a little about their next steps. Then Piers said, "What do you want to do about Mrs. Robb?"

April took her hands off his knee and dropped a kiss on it. Piers wondered how much time they had for privacy before dinner.

"Talk to her. First. Let's get it over with."

Chapter Seven

As expected, they found Mrs. Robb in April's dressing room. The baby lay in her lap, half-asleep, while she fastened the bodice of her gown. Clearly, she had just fed him. The knowledge raised a few hairs on the back of Piers's neck, probably because this was April's room. Just for an instant, he imagined April feeding her own baby, *his* baby.

Would she miss it if she never had that opportunity? Would he?

Yes, he would. But it had always been April that was important. Heirs were considered his duty as the viscount, but in truth they were a very distant priority. If his career had remained in Oxford, he would never have married. And marrying April had been nothing to do with heirs. So far as he was concerned, even if his cousin Bertie, his current heir, curled up his toes on the Peninsula, there were still other, more distant cousins to fill his shoes.

April had told him she couldn't have children because of a past that he hated to think about and she had mostly forgotten. She minded for his sake, not for her own. Or so he had always believed until he saw her gaze not on Mrs. Robb but on the baby in her lap.

The wet nurse rose calmly to her feet, the baby comfortably in one arm. She curtseyed. "My lord. My lady."

"Mrs. Robb," Piers said civilly. "How is your charge?"

"He feeds well, my lord. He's a very good baby."

"I'm glad to hear it." On impulse, he walked up to her and took the baby from her. She resisted, clinging for a moment, then dropped her eyes and gave in. *Interesting...*

The baby smelled curiously pleasant, reminding him of something long distant. Another baby encountered in childhood, no doubt. Gussie, perhaps? Or even Maria...

"I was just going to put him down in his cot," Mrs. Robb said firmly. She didn't quite dare to take the child from him again, but he could have sworn her arms twitched in that direction.

"He'll spill out of that box, soon," April remarked. "Do we not have a more suitable cradle in the Nursery, Piers? It would have to be thoroughly cleaned, of course. Or we could buy one."

Piers nodded, though he kept his gaze on the nurse. "Why don't we investigate that tomorrow? Lady Petteril has just been talking to your mother."

Mrs. Robb's eyes widened, flying to April and then back to Piers and to the baby he held. The little boy stirred comfortably, turning his face into Piers's shoulder. Like a puppy, trusting, reliant, and yet horribly vulnerable.

Oh dear...

"My mother?" Mrs. Robb said as though unconcerned. Her eyes said otherwise. "How on earth did that come about?"

"I chose to follow up your character with the agency," April told her. "Which sent me to your old home and then your current one. You lied to the agency and you lied to us."

"I did?" Mrs. Robb was trying to brazen it out, but she knew the axe was falling.

"Your child is not dead. Of that we are very glad. But the lies remain an issue."

Mrs. Robb tilted her chin. "I need the work. My baby doesn't need my milk, so I can feed others and keep the admittedly wretched roof over her head."

"Did someone tell you about this child?" Piers asked, cupping the baby's head to be sure it didn't loll back. His skin was soft, the light down of his hair like silk. "Tell you which agency to register with?"

She shook her head. "No. But I needed a wealthy client. The few pennies I made wet nursing for my working neighbour barely cover the cost of cow's milk. So I went to the most respectable agency I knew of. Not many women like me register to be wet nurses. I thought I might impress someone."

"Oh, you did," April agreed. "You impressed the agency, and Mrs. Park. And his lordship and me—until we discovered the lies."

Mrs. Robb met her gaze. "Would you have engaged me if you'd known I had a baby of my own at home? Knowing I'd abandoned her?"

"With your mother," April said with a twitch of the brow.

"I was going to ask you for half days," Mrs. Robb admitted. "To go home to my daughter and give my mother a rest. I would have taken Georgie with me..."

"Georgie?" Piers asked with an upward twitch of his eyebrow.

Mrs. Robb smiled with a wealth of sorrow as she gazed at the baby once more. "Every child should have a name. It seems even more important for those who're unwanted."

Unwanted. Piers could feel his arm begin to tighten around the baby and forced it to relax. "Well, in the absence of his own name, Georgie will do."

"He's a good baby," Mrs. Robb said, almost desperately. "I can take him home with me. His mother isn't coming back for him now. I'll look after him well, same as my own. They'll be brother and sister..."

"And you'll have two growing mouths to feed as well as your own," April said flatly. Though her eyes were not unkind. They were understanding.

Mrs. Robb had lost her husband and her home. Her only purpose, her only comfort, was clearly in taking care of her baby and other people's.

"Then you didn't see the baby on our step early yesterday morning?" Piers asked her.

Mrs. Robb glanced up and met his gaze, shaking her head without hesitation. "No. I'd never even been to this square before I was sent yesterday afternoon. I didn't know it existed."

Piers met April's gaze. Amanda Robb's defences were down and they both knew the truth when they heard it.

AROUND THE DINNER HOUR was a bad time to question any of the servants since they were all particularly busy. So once changed for dinner, leaving April to look in on his cousin Gussie, Piers returned to the library to contemplate what they knew about the baby—beyond the fact that he was ridiculously tiny and endearing. And from there, how much he should confide in Park.

Deciding it would be cruel to even suggest he might have found Simon until he had some kind of proof, he made plans to return to the hackney stand early the following morning —probably with April, since she would be more likely to perceive any likeness to the Parks and remember who she saw.

Then there was Darcy. Piers wondered if he could get his stable lad, Bernie, to follow the man around for a bit, just to see what he was up to. In the past, Ape had always been useful at that kind of thing...

Gussie strolled into the room, looking about her while Piers poured her a small glass of sherry.

"I like this room now," she remarked. "Before you, it was sadly neglected. Papa only ever used it to meet his stuffier guests."

"Do you miss living here?" he asked curiously, for it had been her home up until a year ago when her mother had made way for Piers who had inherited the title and everything that went with it.

Gussie shook her head. "I thought I would, but I don't. I found I was glad to move out —too much death here—even though Mama hated leaving so much. It's a better house with you and April in it now."

"Is that a compliment?"

She grinned. "Of course it is. Swallow it and say thank you."

"Thank you," he said politely. "Where did you leave April?"

"Oh, with the baby! Isn't he adorable? And just think, Maria's must be even tinier!"

WHEN THE LADIES WITHDREW from the dining room after dinner, Piers regarded the port decanter without much interest. It was not a great deal of fun drinking without company after dinner, so when they had no guests, he generally just accompanied April to the drawing room or the library.

For appearance, he poured himself a glass, then rose and pulled the bell.

Joshua appeared a few moments later. He was a few years older than Francis and had darker hair.

"Send Francis to me, would you?" Piers said, and stretched his legs out under the table, crossing them at the ankles. He had done a fair bit of walking today and his feet were tired.

Francis appeared very sharply, without his usual grin. His expression was wary, as if he expected to be punished for something.

"My lord?" he said, bowing.

"Close the door."

Wary changed to *alarmed*, but the lad obeyed without question.

"Francis," Piers said, "as you know, we have a baby problem."

"It's not mine, my lord," Francis blurted.

"Why on earth should I imagine it is?"

"Because everyone knows I've got a sweetheart in Mrs. Renton's employ."

"*Still* in Mrs. Renton's employ?" Piers asked delicately.

"Of course, my lord."

The words should have been a comfort, for no one would retain a pregnant maid, yet Francis's uneasy manner remained. He wasn't quite shuffling from foot to foot but only because he had been trained not to.

"Do we have a different problem, Francis?"

"No, my lord. Everything is under control."

"Is it?" Piers said slowly. "And yet I think you had better tell me." He cast around for a more encouraging phrase. "Man to man. Rather than Lady Petteril finding out from other sources."

Francis did shift feet then. "There's nothing to find out," he said pleadingly. "Or at least not yet. Truth is, Emma and me.... Well, Emma thinks she might be—it's possible but not likely, only she's missed... I'd marry her, my lord, I would, only I couldn't stay with you, then, and she'd lose her position, and we'd have no work between us. What sort of start is that for a child?"

"For any of you," Piers agreed. He sat up, frowning. "Look, the matter is not beyond redemption, even if Emma proves to be increasing. You are *not* to let her try and be rid of it for she's more likely to kill herself, whatever happens to her child. *Your* child," he added with an extra glare, just in case Francis felt any inclination to shrug off the responsibility that would never affect his life as it did the mother's.

Francis dropped his eyes. To give him his due, there was anguish in his face.

"You will promise me," Piers said sternly—and just a little hypocritically—"to keep your breeches buttoned until you can afford the luxury of a wife and child. For now, should Emma be certain, I'll try and find you work as a couple, but it won't be the sort of career you're hoping for. Just set her mind at rest so that she does nothing silly."

"Yes, my lord. I *do* promise! Thank you..."

Piers picked up his glass. "Don't thank me yet. You'll make a rotten farmer."

"IF FRANCIS DOES HAVE a child," Piers said to April when they were finally alone in his bedchamber, "it is not yet born. He and Mrs. Renton's maid appear to be at the stage of crossing their fingers and praying."

"Oh dear," April said. Her blue eyes were almost navy blue in the candlelight and as ancient as the sky. "We can't..." She broke off.

"I know," Piers said, sitting down on the chair by his dressing table which was scattered now with her things—hairbrushes and pins and perfume bottles and mysterious little jars which she delighted in because they were pretty and she had never had such fripperies before. "I made it clear we were the alternative to the girl's last resort."

April peered at him curiously, distracted from the matter in hand. "How do you know?"

"About supposed wise-women and so-called doctors in back streets? I don't recall. Hearsay." He knew she would have seen the result from much closer. Loosening his cravat, he said, "I tried to scare Francis into some responsibility—despite having avoiding all such at his age—but it is hardly my forte."

Her lip twitched. "More than you know. Your disfavour is terrifying."

"Is it?" he asked, startled.

She came and sat on his knee in a flurry of skirts, looping her arms around his neck and kissing his cheek—by way of answer, presumably. "So, we can rule out Francis and his sweetheart."

"And from what Gussie said over dinner, there have been no servant crises or recent changes of any kind at my aunt's house." He put one arm around her waist, while he dropped his cravat on the table.

She began to unfasten his sleeve buttons. "I spoke to Smithy the maid as well. She confirms it."

He mentioned his idea for looking further into Darcy, and she nodded agreement.

"Maybe I should speak to Annie as well, see what she has heard."

Annie was her old friend from urchin days, who had risen from street prostitution to a home of her own and an aristocratic protector—who had, sadly, been murdered. Annie still had possession of the house, though, and a new protector who lavished gifts upon her.

"By all means." A spurt of frustration made him scowl. "But of all the hundreds of unwanted or impossible-to-care-for babies in London, why did *this* one end up on *our* doorstep?"

"There doesn't have to be a connection, Piers. Some things just happen from chance, without reason."

She was right, of course. And that meant they might never trace the baby's origins. Which would leave them with a whole new set of problems.

With his sleeve buttons removed, she rested her head on his shoulder, and he held her in silence. He had the feeling they were both thinking of the baby who slept so close to them, of what life could possibly have in store for him now. Dangerous thoughts. But so curiously warm and woolly that he wanted to go and say goodnight to "Georgie". To stand by his makeshift cradle and watch him sleep.

IN THE QUIET OF THE night, Piers lay beside April and heard the distant cry of the hungry baby. It was only for a moment. Presumably, Mrs. Robb gathered him up at once. The image confused him, muddled as it was with April.

Was it not women who were meant to turn broody at times?

Beside him, April breathed with the evenness of sleep. He rather thought she was broody too. Which was hard and would get harder if they were not blessed with children. But that too would pass.

It was a long time since he had lain awake for so long. But the blackness no longer smothered his mind—or at least it was never more than a passing cloud. It was the mystery of the baby that kept his mind active. Something bothered him about what they knew, or didn't know. He just couldn't quite isolate what it was.

Used to dealing with insomnia, he slipped out of bed, found slippers and his dressing gown and felt his way to the door, grabbing a stump of candle as he went. He did not light it until he had closed the bedroom door behind him and found the flint and tinder box in his sitting room.

Then he crept into the passage and downstairs to the kitchen, where, with a familiarity that might have surprised his servants, especially by the tiny glimmer of his candle, he proceeded to make himself a cup of hot chocolate and to hunt out one of Mrs. Gale's delicious butter biscuits.

Eventually, he sat at the kitchen table, munching his biscuit and sipping his chocolate, and remembering the night he had done so with April, when she was still his servant, and had scared him witless by vanishing alone into her old haunts in an effort to solve a very different sort of crime. No one but he had ever looked after her.

But then, she looked after him.

He smiled into his hot chocolate, letting the happiness that still astonished him wrap around his heart and mind. He wouldn't let the current mystery into his thoughts just yet. It was waiting its turn, to be considered afresh.

The quiet sound did not even startle him. At first, he even thought it was part of his memory of that night when he had waited for April to come home.

But she *was* home, and no one should be trying to unlock the area door at this time of night.

He sprang up, his heart lurching. Again, he seized his single candle, carrying it with him to the narrow passage that led to the area door. Leaving the light just inside the kitchen, he crept his way to the door, from where a surreptitious, metallic scraping sounded. Like April picking a lock with one of the tools she had never got around to throwing out.

Whoever was on the other side of the door was less skilled than April. For Piers, curiosity had often overcome wariness—and sense—so he did not think twice about giving the would-be housebreaker a helping hand.

On the off-chance that the burglar ever managed to turn the lock, Piers obligingly slid back the bolts. He could hear the breathed curses of the would-be intruder.

It could be a long wait, Piers decided. Since his eyes were used to the dark—more so than the burglar's would be in the glow of the streetlamps outside—he found the shape of the key on the hook without difficulty. He held it poised before the keyhole for a second, while using his other hand to pick up the folded umbrella that was always kept in the corner by the door.

Then he slipped the key into the lock. He shoved hard, pushing out whatever flimsy tools were in there, turned the key and wrenched open the door. Instantly, he jabbed the umbrella point outward, apparently into the neck of the dark figure still kneeling there.

The man—at least it sounded like a man—made a horrible gurgling noise and fell over.

Piers, who had not expected his exploratory jab to be quite so effective, had already adopted a defensive position with the umbrella held horizontally before him. It wasted a precious moment which the would-be intruder used to leap to his feet and, instead of attacking, he fled ignominiously. His feet pounded up the area steps.

Piers hared after him, umbrella at the ready, dressing gown flapping about him, reminding him that beneath it he was stark naked. Fortunately, since it was so early in the year, the streets were quiet, but still, the sight of Lord Petteril's bare legs flying down the street after a fleeing man was not one he cared to leave in people's minds. Though it was probably exquisitely funny. *Too eccentric by far, my dear...*

Fighting laughter now, he tried to tighten the dressing gown belt while continuing to run, and lost even more ground to his quarry, who swerved suddenly into the lane that led to the mews. Piers charged after him, but by the time he reached the mews itself, he heard the sound of galloping hooves and the jingling of a carriage harness. Although he ran after it, he knew both carriage and housebreaker were lost to him, disappearing at high speed into the night.

Annoyed by what he knew was his own clumsiness, Piers marched briskly back to the front of his house before a more enterprising burglar took advantage of the open door.

At the foot of the area steps, April stood in the doorway, looking beautiful and angelically concerned in the golden glow of the lamp she held.

"Piers?" she hissed.

"Alone and defeated," he murmured, descending the steps.

She stepped back, clearly impatient to know what had occurred, but as her lamp moved, so did Piers's perception and he caught sight of something small and pale on the ground beside the dust bin. He stooped to pick it up and by the light of April's lamp recognized a slightly wilted and crushed Christmas rose.

"Tucker," he said, pleased.

Chapter Eight

"Tucker?" April repeated, dragging him into the house by the arm before locking and bolting the door behind him.

"The hackney driver I thought might be Simon Park."

"He was here?"

"He wore a flower like this in his buttonhole yesterday."

While they sat at the kitchen table, sharing the remains of his once hot—now vaguely warm—chocolate, he told her about the would-be intruder's unskilled efforts to break in and Piers's even more inept efforts to catch the villain in the act.

She grinned as he had known she would, though she said stoutly. "I don't think you were inept at all. You *did* stop him from breaking in and you discovered who he is. You obviously did rattle him yesterday with your questions. I think he must be Simon Park after all. Though changing his name to Tucker is odd."

She picked up the single flower. "Do you suppose he came to see his parents? Or to explain about the baby?"

"Why wouldn't he just knock on the door at a reasonable hour of the day? He has every right to see his parents."

"But not to abandon a child on our doorstep." Her eyes widened. "He might have come tonight to steal back the baby!"

"Then why abandon him in the first place?"

"Perhaps he only meant to leave Georgie in his parents' care for a while. But you're right, it doesn't quite make sense."

"There *is* sense," Piers said, vaguely. "We're just not seeing it." He shoved the cup in April's direction and folded her hands around it. "You finish it, and then we can go back to bed for a couple of hours…"

APRIL WAS GLAD, THOUGH not surprised, to find out that Bernie, their stable boy, was acquainted with the grooms who worked for the Darcy family. He was therefore despatched to see what he could discover in their stables, and to discreetly follow James Darcy if and when he left the house.

The boy seemed glad of this reprieve from routine—to say nothing of the extra silver surreptitiously dropped into his pocket—so she and Piers returned to the house for breakfast.

Their first stop of the day was to be the Oxford Street hackney stand, where they intended to watch and wait until Tucker of the Christmas rose made an appearance. It was not an infallible plan, since Tucker was likely to see them first. Piers would never remember his face—although the buttonhole might give him away if he was foolish enough to wear one the same flower—and April had never laid eyes on him.

Piers would just have to keep his head down so as to avoid giving the man any clue they were looking for him.

Before they left, April returned to her own bedchamber and made an excuse to look in on Georgie the baby who was feeding, but who kicked his little legs at April's entrance, as though he recognized her. Touched, April smiled at him.

"I thought I might take him for a breath of fresh air in the park this morning," Mrs. Robb said with a hint of defiance—presumably against dismissal. "Well wrapped up, of course, and not if it's raining. Or snowing," she added, glancing out of the window with disfavour.

"Ah. I don't want you to do that," April said. "Someone tried to break into the house last night and his lordship and I are afraid he was trying to steal the baby."

Mrs. Robb blinked. "Seriously? Who *is* this baby?"

"That is what we are trying to find out. But yes, seriously. I don't want either you or Georgie in danger, so please don't take him beyond the garden."

Mrs. Robb frowned, opened her mouth to argue, and then closed it again while the baby released her and gazed in concentration at April.

"Very well," Mrs. Robb said.

A bad smell wafted under April's nostrils. It appeared to explain the infant's focus. "Monstrous little creature," she told him, then pulled herself together and addressed Mrs. Robb. "Take some time this afternoon to visit your own daughter. Bring her back with you," she added recklessly, "if your mother needs to be elsewhere. Hopefully, this uncertainty will not go on too long."

She wasn't quite sure what she meant by that, so she hurried off to see Gussie before she rejoined Piers for their expedition. Gussie, still bleary-eyed, was sitting up in bed with a cup of tea while Smithy fussed over tonics on the bedside table.

"Piers and I will be out all morning, probably, but we can go for a drive or a walk in the park in the afternoon, if you like."

"Perfect," Gussie replied.

"Um... If, for some reason, we're not back for luncheon, could you keep an eye on the baby? Mrs. Robb has a half-day. Sort of."

Gussie blinked. "What do I do with him?"

"Oh, just watch him sleep," April said optimistically. "And send for Mrs. Park if he won't stop crying. Or if he stinks," she added with a bright smile.

Gussie giggled behind her as she whisked out of the room.

Although April had grown used to walking in public on her husband's arm, today, for some reason, it felt very strange again. Or perhaps it was she who felt strange. It was certainly very pleasant, and she knew she looked the part of the viscountess in her fashionable fur-trimmed pelisse and matching hat. She had learned to walk with poise so that she did not disgrace him.

Where were these thoughts coming from? They had both gone into this unequal marriage with their eyes open, knowing what they would face from others, but also—at least from September—the value they held for each other. She might be an inadequate viscountess, but however amazing it might be, she was very necessary to the viscount.

The odd feelings she was trying to throw off were, she supposed, just another stage of adjustment to her new life.

Distracting herself, she said cheerfully, "I don't want to neglect poor Gussie, so I've said I'll go for a drive with her this afternoon."

"Good plan. We might find we have morning callers too, now that she is with us."

"Meaning Haggs?" April said, referring to his friend Sir Peter Haggard, who seemed to have developed a soft spot for Gussie.

"Or any other of her flirts."

"*Is* she just flirting with Haggs?" April asked. "She is *different* with him."

"Matters will take their natural course," Piers said vaguely.

The usual three stalls were set up at the corner opposite the park, with both pies and vegetables being in demand. Flowers, not so much, but then the flower barrow was almost hidden by the taller bigger pie stall. And the girl huddled there looked unhappy to the point of devastation. A momentary expression, April thought with relief as the girl smiled at them around Jack Newly's large shoulder.

"Morning, sir," Newly called. "Lovely warm pie to eat in the park?"

"Not right now, thank you," Piers said cheerfully.

The flower girl's gaze darted all around. Her whole body was poised and yet rigid.

"She's frightened," April said. "More frightened. Piers, is Jack Newly trying to squeeze her out of her patch?"

"Shouldn't think so. They're not in competition."

"Then why is she hidden behind him, almost invisible to the passing trade? She's got little enough to sell as it is."

Piers, who always listened to her, took another look. His brow tugged into a quick frown. "Perhaps we should buy flowers on the way back. Shall we walk through the Green Park to avoid the worst of the Piccadilly traffic?"

***

THE STAND IN OXFORD Street had several hackneys lined up waiting. While Piers pretended to be looking at shop windows as an excuse to hide his face—his strange affliction of face-blindness meant he was very unlikely to recognize anyone he spoke to yesterday for the first time—April gazed toward the jarveys, searching out buttonholes or any sign of unease as they strolled past.

But none of the drivers tried to hide their own faces or showed any expression of alarm. April and Piers reached the end of the line of carriages, after which April pretended to have missed the shop she had come for and dragged Piers back toward an elegant window of hats and gloves.

This time, Piers leaned his back idly against the window, showing his face to any who cared to look. He even pushed his hat back at a rakish angle on his head.

"Our man might bolt," April murmured.

"In which case, we'll bolt too. A pity we can't drive them ourselves..."

The line of hackneys moved up as the front one was taken. Another joined the back of the line.

"Someone's saluting me with his whip," Piers said, touching the brim of his hat in response.

Quickly, April followed his gaze. It was the jarvey at the back of the line. "No buttonhole that I can see. Bulky cove—his coat buttons are stretched. He doesn't have much hair."

"I did speak to a bald fellow yesterday," Piers said, straightening, and drawing her hand back through his arm. "Brearly by name. Let's stroll in his direction."

As they did so, the jarvey at the back grinned and doffed his hat to reveal an entirely bald pate. "Morning, guv'nor!" he called. "Found who abandoned that kid yet?"

Piers moved nearer to him. "Sadly not. But something did come up that I wanted to speak to that other driver about—your friend with the Christmas rose in his buttonhole complaining about families making his cab sticky. Tucker, I think you said."

The man grinned. "Amos? Grumpy sod—begging your pardon, ma'am—when he wants to be but no harm in him."

"Doesn't he have children of his own then?" April asked innocently.

"Couldn't tell you that, ma'am. He's got a wife, though. Talks about her sometimes." A curious expression crossed his face that April couldn't quite understand. Doubt? Disapproval?

"I don't see him here today," Piers said. "Will you tip me the wink if you see him first?"

"'Course I will," Brearly said generously. "If I'm still waiting." As the carriage in front eased forward a few steps, his horse ambled forward too without obvious instruction. April and Piers moved with him. "Wait though," he said suddenly, taking off his hat again and scratching his scalp. "He ain't working today. I saw him on my way to work this morning —in the street like. Looked pretty rough too, poor bug—er... fellow."

"You mean he's sick?" Piers asked in surprise, though it wasn't really astonishing if a man poked in the throat with an umbrella should feel a trifle unwell the next day.

"Looked it," the jarvey replied.

"I don't suppose you know where he lives?" Piers said hopefully.

Their informant shrugged, abruptly closing ranks with his absent colleague against the nosy nobs. "I don't go round for tea and scones."

"No matter," Piers said. "I can easily find out from the borough records."

"That's true," the man allowed, perhaps feeling his refusal had been too hasty. He stared at Piers. "I don't hold with abandoning children. Terrible thing to do."

"It is," April said cordially. "Which is why my husband needs Mr. Tucker's help."

"He's not in trouble," Piers assured him.

Yet, thought April grimly.

"I need to know about one of his passengers," Piers continued. "You can't pick and choose those, after all."

"Wish you could sometimes," the jarvey said with feeling. "I been doing this for close on five years now and—"

"Same as Mr. Tucker?" April interrupted.

"Nah, he's a Johnny-come-lately. Look, I don't know his precise direction but I can tell you roughly. Save you going to the borough."

"That's very helpful of you," Piers said fervently.

"A wife," April murmured, as they made their way to the front of the line of hackney cabs. "Do you suppose Simon took the mother as well as the child when he fled from the north?"

"It's possible. It would certainly be another reason to hide from his disapproving parents. Only why would he leave the child now? Why would she?"

"Maybe she died," April said with sudden bleakness.

"There is no reason to suppose so." He spoke with perfect calm but as though he understood her sudden surge of unspecific grief, he covered her hand with his. And then they were climbing into the front carriage and heading for Amos Tucker's neighbourhood.

AMANDA ROBB WALKED out of the back door into the kitchen garden, another woman's child in her arms when she longed for her own.

Not that she resented this scrap of abandoned humanity. It was the parents she resented. How could they leave their child with strangers?

The Petterils, of course, were rich people. Kind people, too, apparently. But surely whoever left the boy on their doorstep hadn't cared about that. They had just left him and run. Indefensible.

The sky was quite clear this morning, the sunshine bright though cold. She walked around the garden with Georgie, telling him about the herbs they passed, and the apple tree and gooseberry bushes. Georgie looked as though he were interested.

On Lady Petteril's orders, an old but beautiful cradle had been rescued from a dusty room at the top of the house and was being thoroughly cleaned. In their own way these people were looking after Georgie. His lordship was not immune to the baby's appeal.

As for her ladyship... Amanda was more worried about her. Like herself, Lady Petteril would find it hard to let go when she had to. And she *would* have to. Even if his lordship decided to pay for Georgie's upbringing, it would never be as their son. Titled lords needed blood heirs. They would have children of their own and forget about Georgie.

I wouldn't. But then, Amanda had no chance now of other children. Her husband was dead, and she could not imagine marrying again. She sat down dreamily on the wrought iron bench, lifting her face to the weak sunshine. *But I could take him in. With the Petteril's recommendation, I could get other positions with rich people, afford a better place for Mama and Esther and Georgie...*

Only she would not see her daughter as often as she wished... Like now, and it had only been a day. She looked forward to going home quite fiercely, even for an hour or two...

Her skin prickled and she opened her eyes, instinctively holding the baby closer. Lady Petteril had been afraid someone was trying to steal Georgie... Amanda had thought it foolish imagination, yet now she gazed around, at each of the blank windows of the house. From the kitchen sink, the maid Janey waved to her.

But still the hairs on Amanda's neck stood up. Someone was watching her. She knew it.

A breeze ruffled the bare branches of the apple tree. The gooseberry bushes suddenly seemed too thick and impenetrable, the garden too vulnerable.

Abruptly, she stood and almost ran along the path back into the house.

IN THE END, PIERS AND April found Tucker's abode without having to ask. It was the only one that boasted an outbuilding that had clearly been used as a stable and carriage house. And right in front of that was a lushly blooming Christmas rose bush.

"There's no horse or carriage in the stable," April said, after jumping up to see in the cracked and grimy window. "If he isn't at work, where is he?"

"I have a horrible feeling I know," Piers said ruefully. "Let's ask his nearest neighbour."

This turned out to be a young woman with a toddling child clinging to her skirts.

"Mr. Tucker?" she said in reply to Piers's question. "He's gone, sir. He got a new place, cheaper rent and better accommodation for the horse."

"We've just missed him, have we not?"

"Afraid so sir," the young woman said. "He just loaded up the last of the things into the carriage a couple of hours ago and off he went."

"Was his wife with him?" April asked.

"Oh, no, she went already the day before—or was it the day before that?—to make it homely while he did the heavy lifting and caught her up."

"She took the baby, then," April said, making it more statement than question, but the woman nodded as though that was understood.

April was almost bouncing on Piers's arm as they left the neighbour's door. "There *is* a baby," she crowed. "And either of them could have left it on our doorstep."

"But why would they?" Piers asked. "These are decent lodgings and he looked well enough and prosperous enough to me."

"She left him," April said. "Tucker is Simon and he left the baby on our doorstep for his parents to look after."

It was, Piers reflected, the only story that made sense. Only the secrecy seemed wrong —breaking into Petteril House whether to get the baby back or to speak to the Parks. "I suppose prison might have made him secretive... He might have lurked some time in his cab outside our house, wondering if he'd done the right thing, and then bolted suddenly before he changed his mind, going so fast that he knocked Darcy over on the way past."

She glanced at him sharply. "You don't believe it."

"I don't disbelieve it. I just don't think we have all the facts."

"We certainly don't have Simon," she allowed, frowning. "Nor any forwarding address for him. More prison secrecy?"

"Perhaps. Either way, we have lost him for the day. He won't be back at the hackney stand until tomorrow."

"He won't be able to afford missing too many days work," April said. "Shall we go home to Gussie?"

"Via a couple of men's hostels," Piers said. "Just in case Tucker is *not* Simon."

PETTERIL'S BABY

GUSSIE WAS WANDERING aimlessly around her old home, which now looked and felt so different, willing herself back to health and looks. A little fresh air might give her back some bloom...

She turned her steps toward the kitchen, thinking she could sit on the garden bench, if it was not too cold, and read a chapter of her novel. From the foot of the kitchen stairs, she could either go into the kitchen itself, or the narrow passage that led between the back door and the area door. Judging by the laughter and the cooing coming from the kitchen, the baby and his temporary nurse were in there. Gussie hesitated a moment, for she liked babies and had better grow used to them too before she met her nephew.

But fresh air beckoned first. She could worship at the baby shrine after that. Before she could reach for the back door, a knock sounded on the area door—loud enough to be heard by the kitchen staff had they not all been occupied in gushing and chortling over the baby.

Even Gussie's footsteps in the passage, moving all the way from the back to the front of the house did not disturb them. Gussie opened the area door to find a very small woman in black at the door. Black hat, black veil, black cloak.

"Good morning," said this diminutive, funereal vision in an anxious, sorrowful voice. "I have come about the baby."

"The baby?" Gussie repeated, startled.

"The one that was found on your doorstep," the woman said. Behind the veil, her eyes glittered with emotion. "It's mine."

Gussie caught her breath. "You had better come in," she said. What a pity Piers and April had chosen this morning to go out! And then, with a little more glee, it struck her that for once, *she* would be solving their puzzle for *them*.

"Oh, I can hear the little mite!" the woman exclaimed, all but rushing past Gussie to the near kitchen door, where she was brought up short by the solid, impressive figure of Park, who looked over her head at Gussie.

"Is this person known to you, Miss Withan?" he inquired in the lofty way only butlers could.

"No, but she says the baby is hers..."

Park looked down his nose at the woman with an unexpected lack of kindness. "Madam?"

"Let me see my dear little Charlie," she begged.

"Perhaps, when you tell me precisely which step you left the child on."

"Bless, you," whispered the woman, raising a handkerchief to her veiled eyes with more symbolism that practicality. "It was not I who left him. It was my stepdaughter, just to vex her husband and her papa, knowing little Charlie is the apple of both their eyes."

"Then the child is not yours but your stepdaughter's?" Mrs. Park said, from beside her husband. Behind them, quite a crowd of servants had formed, though not Mrs. Robb. And not the first footman, Joshua, who stood now at the back door, while the other footman, Francis, paused on his way down the steps from above.

Behind her veil, the visitor's eyes seemed to flicker, taking it all in. "My step-daughter's, to my shame. It took us this long to get the truth out of her."

"She does not sound a fit person to be caring for the child," Gussie said indignantly.

"Oh, she isn't, miss, she isn't. Which is why *I* shall be taking care of it from now on."

That seemed a much better idea to Gussie. Surely Piers would be happier about it too...

The woman took a hesitant step toward Park. "So if you will just..."

"But we will not *just* hand the child over," Park said with quite unnecessary hauteur. "You come back with the child's parents when Lord Petteril is here, and he will discuss the matter."

The veiled woman's eyes sparked through the veil—grief or anger? Either way, Gussie could not blame her. She had never seen the kind-hearted Park so...*hard*.

"You can't just abduct a child!" the woman said, rallying, with threat in her voice.

"Nor can you abandon it on a doorstep for days. But if we're talking about the law, I'm sure his lordship will be happy to bring along a magistrate to decide the legalities, once all the witnesses are gathered."

"You break my heart," the woman mourned. "You break my husband's heart!"

"The matter may be resolved as I have outlined," Park said, moving inexorably forward so that the visitor had to fall back to the area door, which he opened with perfect civility.

"Cruel," the woman whispered. "Too cruel."

He was, and the indignant Gussie couldn't understand it.

"Good day, madam." Park almost pushed her out by closing the door, which he locked and bolted behind her.

Chapter Nine

Piers felt somewhat frustrated, not to say outwitted, by the slippery Amos Tucker, who had certainly eluded them most effectively. Unsure of the regulations, he didn't know if Tucker could simply choose to work from a different hackney stand. Or sell his horse and carriage and vanish into London's anonymity.

Which really didn't sound like any son of the Parks, even one who had been to prison.

So how could his questions at the stand the previous day have stirred Tucker to house-breaking? Was the Christmas rose a misleading clue? Or was Tucker truly the father of the child trying to steal it back? Then why abandon his son in the first place?

"We are going in circles," he said abruptly, climbing back into the hackney after asking questions at the third hostel he had visited that morning.

"Slowly."

April was irritated because he was insisting on going alone into these insalubrious hostels. If they had separated, they could have got round twice as many. In the old days, as Ape or April, she could have been much more effective in such investigations, inveigling all sorts of people to talk to her. He had rather tied her hands by making her Lady Petteril and she knew it.

If she had been Hortensia, she would have sniffed. As it was, she glared at him, shifting restlessly.

"I don't even hold the horses anymore," she muttered as the hackney moved on.

He nudged her with his elbow. "If it's any consolation, I feel I've been wasting my own time too. I'm beginning to wonder if either Tucker or Simon, even if they're the same man, have anything to do with our baby. Maybe it's time to *think*. And to write."

Piers had always been an intellectual, a man of thought. That he could also be effective as a man of action had been something of a revelation that helped him deal with the difficult transition from Oxford don to viscount. And to solve new kinds of puzzles. But sometimes he did need space—and peace—to clarify his mind and see the truth.

April, since she had first learned to use a pen, had begun to write things down. She thought and acted quickly because she had always had to, but often their joint clarity had come from what she had written.

She nodded and leaned against him. "It must be midday anyway. We should go home to Gussie."

"I already told the jarvey."

They were quiet on the journey home, but silence with April had always been as pleasant as her sunny chatter.

Only, over the last few days, she hadn't seemed quite as sunny as usual. Glancing at her, he saw her eyelids drooping and closing. Of course, her sleep had been interrupted last night by his blundering pursuit of their house breaker.

The familiar, gentle ache of protective love folded around him. There were many joys in marriage, he had found. And there were these quiet, profound moments he had no name for.

In the traffic confusion of Piccadilly, the hackney was forced to halt behind a large dray whose driver was arguing vociferously, though with whom, Piers could not see. What did make him sit up was the sight of his neighbour, James Darcy, weaving along Piccadilly toward St. James as though with some purpose. And a few yards behind him, bless his heart, weaved the quick, casually slouching figure of Bernie, Petteril's new stable boy.

Good for you, lad.

As though his involuntary movement had woken her, April lifted her head from his shoulder. The hackney moved forward to the sound of a few more insults hurled by their driver.

"Darcy," Piers explained. "With young Bernie on his tail."

"Oh." She stretched and blinked rapidly. "I need to wake myself up. Can we walk from here?"

"Why not?" Piers rapped with his cane on the roof and heard the jarvey curse as he manoeuvred into a safe place to halt.

Piers alighted, handed down his sleepy lady, and paid the grumpy driver before strolling on toward home with her hand in his arm. Someone raised his hat to them, which Piers acknowledged with a gracious nod and walked on, since he'd no idea who the man was.

Neither had April, apparently, for she did not murmur his name as she always did if she knew.

Newly the pie-man's stall had been re-stocked for the midday rush, and he was doing a brisk trade. Reg the Veg was not short of customers either.

"The flower girl's gone," April said beside him. "Why is she always hidden or gone?"

She veered toward the stalls, dragging Piers with her. He gave in, since she had a point. She caught Reg's attention just by her presence, and being so clearly above the rank of the others who surrounded him.

"Where's the flower girl?" April asked him.

"Gone home," said Reg, gesturing toward the empty barrow that stood close into the railings. "Nothing left to sell."

"But she's left her barrow."

"Jack will take it for her."

Will he, by God? Piers regarded the pie man with an interest that wasn't quite free of suspicion, though of what he was at a loss to grasp. Jack Newly was far too busy to notice.

April allowed Piers to draw her away toward home but there was a furrow on her brow that amounted to worry. "I don't like this, Piers. That girl is too frightened."

Once, she had said the same thing about Gussie and she had been right at the time. Because of her, they were all a little wiser. April knew pretty much everything about fear and she recognized the signs most people would never even notice.

"Of what?" he asked. "Those two?"

"They're pushing her out, aren't they? I don't know why, but something is going on. I hate that they can do that, Piers. It isn't right."

He caught her gaze. "I know. But you can't save them all, April."

But she wouldn't be April if she didn't try, now that she was a viscountess with comparative wealth and status. He suspected she had always tried, even when her power was limited to sending the bad men in the wrong direction or just getting in the way and being cuffed aside for her pains.

His stomach still tightened at such thoughts. Worse were the sudden tears filling her eyes. She looked away, glaring straight ahead to dissipate them. He allowed her the dignity, giving her a moment's silence before wondering aloud what Gussie was up to.

"Primping in case her admirers call, probably," April said lightly, and the moment passed.

Francis admitted them to the house and took their outerwear with great willingness. His gaze was a mixture of anxiety and hope when it landed on Piers, but that was no bad thing.

"Where is Miss Gussie?" he asked.

"Sitting in the drawing room, my lord."

Gussie was, in fact, *pacing* in the drawing room, and ready to pounce.

"Piers!" she exclaimed, advancing on them from the window. "We know where the baby comes from, and you need to speak to Park who has behaved atrociously!"

Piers blinked. "*Park* has?"

"The baby?" April asked urgently at the same time. "Where is he?"

"Upstairs with the nurse, since she hasn't gone out yet and Park wouldn't let the child's family take him home!"

Piers pointed to the sofa. "Sit, little coz, and stop working yourself into a frenzy that will make you ill again."

April sat beside her and Piers swung over a chair and sat astride it, his arms resting along its back.

"Cough," he suggested.

"What?" Gussie asked, bewildered.

"More than his accent has slipped," April said wryly. "He means, tell us what happened. Who is this family you think is Georgie's?"

"A woman came to the door—the tradesmen's door—while the staff were all drooling over the baby. I was on my way to sit in the garden, and I seemed to be the only person who heard the knock, so I answered it. The woman said she'd come about the baby, so naturally I brought her inside."

"Was she alone?" April asked quickly.

"Quite alone, and she told this most tragic tale of her dreadful stepdaughter who left her own child on a random stranger's doorstep simply to hurt her husband and father! She would not even tell her family where she had abandoned it until they got it out of her today and this lady came at last to fetch him home. Can you imagine the worry? And Park..."

"What was her name?" Piers interrupted.

"Her name?" Gussie closed her mouth, frowning. "Actually, I don't believe she said."

"Don't you find that a little odd?" Piers asked gently.

"What I find odd," Gussie retorted, "is Park's totally unfeeling response! And Mrs. Park backed him up. It was as if they didn't *want* the baby's real family to be found, as if they wanted to keep him for themselves! Honestly, Piers, no one but me even *tried* to stand up for the poor woman who was not even allowed to *see* the baby! Oh, I'm not saying he should go back to his mother who must be utterly unsuitable, but her stepmother will be taking over the care now and she was clearly—"

"Clearly?" April interrupted. "Could you see this woman's face?"

"Well, not exactly..."

"Because she was wearing a black veil?" April said. "And a black hat and cloak? Little woman with a soft voice and a peculiar way of talking?"

Gussie's jaw dropped. "You *know* her?"

"Essie Brown," April said matter-of-factly. "She's a baby farmer."

"A what?"

"She collects babies and children. Some are stolen. Some people pay her—a great deal in some cases—to look after their accidental offspring. Which she does up to a point. Some she sells—again for a great deal of money—to desperate childless couples. Some die because they're too young or get ill and she never lets a doctor over the door. Those who grow big enough she sells into employment—often of a kind you don't even want to know about—or just takes all their wages which amounts to far more than the meagre rations they're given to eat."

She broke off, as though suddenly mindful of her audience and glanced surreptitiously at Piers, who was thinking grimly of the kinds of "employment" she meant.

"That is horrific," Gussie whispered.

"It is," April agreed.

"How do you know these things?" Gussie asked helplessly.

April cast her a wry look Piers knew only too well. He was also painfully sure he knew the answer before she spoke. "In this case because I dodged her and her minions myself for some time—till they decided I was too wild to be tamed. She's a nasty old crow and Park was quite right to eject her."

From the door, which he had entered silently, Park said, "Thank you, my lady. I told her to come back with witnesses and said that Lord Petteril would bring the magistrate. I'm confident we shall never see her again."

Gussie scowled at him. "How did *you* know?"

"She was *wrong*. One develops an instinct over the years."

"Will I?" Gussie asked dispiritedly.

"Probably not to that extent," Piers said. "Which is why you will always have someone like Park to sniff out the bad apples. Thank you, Park. And thank you, Gussie, for giving me another idea."

"What?" Gussie and April demanded at once.

"I'll tell you over luncheon," Piers said.

"Which is now served, my lady," Park said and withdrew.

BERNIE THE STABLE BOY was enjoying himself hugely. Not only was he spared mucking out in the stables, but he got to lounge around the other mews, engaging other lads and indoor servants in idle conversation while he mooched around and pretended to compare masters.

In fact, he was sure no one's master compared to his. Lord Petteril *looked* like a gent. When Bernie had first seen him, he had frozen and quaked in his shoes at what he had perceived as his lordship's haughty magnificence. He had lived in terror of displeasing him in case the godlike creature dismissed him with one careless flick of his long finger.

But then his lordship had addressed him like a human being, overlooked a clumsiness, always said thank you—*thank you!*—and smiled so that Bernie, like the rest of the staff, was devoted. Mostly, Bernie suspected, his lordship didn't even know that.

Her ladyship was a different kettle of fish. Bernie had heard the rumours, of course, that she'd been born no better than him and had once been a servant. After he was cuffed for making a joke about her, he kept his lips resentfully buttoned about her.

But then he found her in the stable one day, feeding carrots and even sugar to the horses, and murmuring nonsense into their receptive ears. That she liked horses had been enough for him to throw off his resentment. The conspiratorial grin she had given him had won his heart. He didn't care where she'd been born, and clearly neither did his lordship. It was all fine with Bernie.

So, he was perfectly happy listening to stories of other, lesser masters and mistresses. He didn't gossip about his own, merely said a word or two and then listened, which was all most folk wanted of you anyway. He learned more than he ever wanted to about several of the neighbours. And he learned that Mr. James Darcy was a top rank wastrel.

Oddly, his grooms were quite proud of the fact he got jug-bitten every night and had the naughtiest and prettiest of lady friends. Rolled home at dawn most mornings. Except for the last couple of nights when he had been in bed before midnight. His valet was, apparently, afraid his master was ill.

Since his quarry was expected to go out around midday, Bernie sauntered off with an airy wave and lounged about the square instead until, sure enough, Mr. Darcy emerged from his front door and walked briskly toward the park. Bernie slouched after him.

Darcy did cast quite a long look at Petteril House, which Bernie thought interesting, and at a hackney driving by at snail's pace, but he didn't stop, merely kept on to Piccadilly where the crowds conveniently hid Bernie, though they also tended to hide Darcy, whom he almost lost twice before he turned into St. James and walked into one of the buildings. Bernie loitered outside.

It was a gentleman's club, judging by the doorman and the number of idle nobs ambling in and rolling out. Some of them were positively bosky by two in the afternoon.

Oddly enough, Darcy didn't seem to be. He waved off his friends, who seemed eager to drag him off somewhere else. Darcy however, held firm, causing one of his friends to exclaim, "It's a woman. Has to be."

"Who is she, Darce?" one of the others called roguishly after him.

Darcy merely raised his hand again without turning.

Bernie eased himself off the lamppost and shambled after him, kicking a stray stone as he went.

A hand fell on his shoulder, making him jerk violently to be free, though the hand held on with ease. "Here, boy."

One of Darcy's friends was waving a silver coin in front of his face, so he stopped struggling. "Follow that fellow in the grey hat and see where he goes. Come and tell me here same time tomorrow, and I'll give you another."

Bernie snatched the coin and grinned. "Thank you, my lord!" he said and walked faster, kicking the stone harder and leaving Darcy's friends guffawing and speculating behind him.

Darcy, however, appeared to be going home for he walked back along Piccadilly the way he had come. At the last moment, he swerved and entered Hyde Park by the Cumberland Gate.

Bernie hoped for some nefarious meeting, or at least an assignation, but none appeared to be forthcoming. Darcy merely walked, then sat on a bench so suddenly that Bernie was forced to walk past him. He was too afraid of giving himself away to glance back, but his shoulders were itching in case Darcy disappeared while he wasn't looking.

In the end, he paused against a tree as if for a rest and glanced back. Darcy's grey hat still lurked above the same bench. *Phew*. In a little, the man stood up and sauntered out of the park by a different gate into Park Lane and walked home.

Only he didn't quite make it home. He turned up the steps of Petteril House and knocked at the door.

Bernie sped up, walked past him for the second time, then ran as fast as he could for the mews and the back way into the house.

Chapter Ten

What Piers said over luncheon, that baby Georgie could have been rescued or stolen from Essie Brown or someone like her, appalled April, though she had to admit it was possible. Quite how and why the baby had been left at Petteril House in particular, remained a mystery. But it now seemed possible that the elusive Tucker could be the hero rather than the villain of the story.

She and Piers just had the vile prospect of trawling through Essie's "farm" and others to investigate.

That, April knew only too well, would be horrific and dangerous and very likely not even productive. And would any children they rescued have any better chance in the orphanages?

Some, she thought. At least the orphanages were founded on some kind of good intention…

Immediately after luncheon, she went up to change her dress—largely an excuse to catch Mrs. Robb before she went out to visit her own family.

The nurse, whose coat and hat lay on her couch, had clearly just finished feeding Georgie and was settling him down to sleep.

"Someone came looking for him," she threw quietly at April.

"Her name is Essie Brown and she's a baby farmer."

Mrs. Robb, who was after all a respectable young woman, blinked as if she had never heard the term before. Then her eyes widened. "You mean…? I thought such creatures were myths."

"Oh, no. They exist. Any way to make money exists. I want you to know in case she or anyone like her approaches you to hand Georgie over."

"It must have been her," Mrs. Robb blurted, gazing fixedly at April. "I took him out into the back garden for some fresh air, and while I was sitting on the bench with him, I just had that feeling of being watched..."

"Did you see anyone?" April asked. "Hear anything?"

"No, I just *felt* it. So I ran back inside, and everyone made a fuss of him until I calmed down. Then that woman came to the door."

"Gussie—my cousin, Miss Withan—said she was quite convincing."

"She did sound distraught. The thing is, my lady, there seems to be so many bad people about with evil motives that it terrifies me in ways I could never have imagined when my husband was alive. How do you ever find the truth in such a-a *web*?"

"Good question," April said ruefully. It struck her that Amanda Robb was not up to snuff, not for living where she did now. To keep her daughter safe, she needed to get out of there, more even than April had needed to get out of St. Giles. Another problem for the future. "We'll manage," she said vaguely. "Go and enjoy your time with your daughter. We'll look after Georgie until you get back."

Mrs. Robb nodded. Reaching for the door, she cast a quick glance over her shoulder at the baby, then went out.

Georgie scrunched up his face and kicked, breathing hard and opening his eyes, as if he sensed his larder had just departed.

"She'll be back, little one," April told him.

He gazed up at her with what felt like trust.

She smiled, touching his soft cheek with her little finger and gently stroking. "Go to sleep, now, Georgie Peorgie." While she kept smiling and stroking, he continued to gaze up at her until his eyes began to close again. Emotion she couldn't name held her captive, but she knew there was care in amongst it, and longing and sorrow and...

And I will not cry. I will not.

All the same, she stayed until Martha the house maid came to sit with him. Even then, she only just managed to remember to change her gown before she went back downstairs to talk to Gussie about their drive.

"Piers has gone to the library," Gussie said, tossing aside her novel with something approaching relief. The girl was clearly bored. "I told him you must be very brave."

"Me? Why?" April asked startled, sitting down opposite her.

"Because you survived what you did. I think *that* shows character, much more than Mama's idea of character which seems to have more to do with blood lines. Like a horse."

April laughed, although she could feel herself blushing. If she was honest, though she knew it would never happen, she wanted Piers's family to accept her, for his sake if no other. "I'm not so different from you. Or your mama. We all deal with the hand we're given and some of us are lucky. Or clever."

Gussie regarded her thoughtfully.

Joshua entered bearing a silver salver and bowed. "Sir Peter Haggard, my lady."

Otherwise known as Haggs, Sir Peter was an old friend of Piers's who was always welcome.

"Oh, show him in," April said at once, aware that Gussie had bounced suddenly to her feet. "And inform his lordship if you would."

Joshua had barely shut the door before Gussie cried in apparent panic, "What the devil is *he* doing here?" She was already halfway across the room, clearly meaning to bolt, which baffled April utterly. The girl wrenched open the drawing room door and was then forced to fall back as Sir Peter strode in.

With the privilege of old friendship and familiarity, he must have simply followed Joshua upstairs.

"Miss Withan," he said, brought up short. He bowed, though his lips twitched with amusement. "I thought you might care to come for a drive in the park since the sun is *almost* shining."

Gussie, after a poor sketch of a curtsey, swung away from him. "How kind," she said distantly. "But I am going later with April."

"We can all go together if you like," he said evenly. He was still smiling though it struck April he was hurt. She liked Sir Peter and could have sworn Gussie did too—a little too much, in fact.

"Not now," Gussie said distantly. She must have realized leaving the room was too rude, so she sat down beside April, holding herself rigid, gazing toward the window.

Baffled, April invited Haggs to sit, which he did. He caught her eye as he did so, his eyebrow twitching in interrogation. She could only shrug minutely. If there was a quarrel between the pair, it was clearly one-sided.

Was this Hortensia's doing? Had the dowager viscountess decided that Haggs was not good enough or rich enough for her daughter? Or was she pushing Gussie towards a marriage the girl was not ready for?

"What's this I hear about a baby on your doorstep?" Sir Peter asked.

"We *thought* the rumour mill would be at full tilt," April said, and at least had something to tell him about until Piers and the tea tray arrived more or less together.

"So," Piers said, while April poured the tea, "if you've heard any un-insulting rumours that might explain the infant being left with us in particular, do enlighten us. Frankly, we are baffled and chasing our tails."

"Surely not," Haggs said sardonically. "We'll allow you a couple more days to resolve the puzzle, will we not, Miss Gussie?"

Gussie, however, had used the receipt of her tea cup as an excuse to move her position and sit well out of Sir Peter's line of direct vision. "Indeed," she said.

"How is Lady Haggard?" April asked after his stepmother largely to avoid the inevitable silence while Piers passed their guest tea and set a plate of dainty sandwiches at his elbow.

"Well. She has left for Pelton Park. I'll be following in a few days since there are several matters there requiring my attention."

Gussie's head moved in an involuntary gesture, as if she was about to look at him, then was still.

Park entered the room with the familiar silver salver, presenting it to April. Surprised, for most of the people in London who were prepared to call on her were already in the room, she picked up the card.

Her gaze flew up to Piers, who was reaching for a scone. "Mr. James Darcy," she said.

He raised his eyebrows, abandoning the scone. "Show him in, Park."

April knew they were both wondering the same thing. Had Bernie the stable lad been caught following him? *Awkward...*

"A neighbour across the square," April told the others.

"Ah. When is it you return to Haybury Court?"

"Tuesday," Piers said, "all being well. We'll take Gussie to Maria's first. I imagine you've heard the good news."

Haggs grinned. "Indeed. My congratulations and good wishes to all Gadsbys."

"Mr. Darcy," Park intoned, and the perfectly tailored yet somehow rakish figure of their neighbour swaggered in and bowed.

Piers went to meet him, his hand held out, while April rose and observed. A few years younger than Piers and Haggs, perhaps still in his early twenties, he already bore lines of excess and dissipation on his face. His eyes, however, were direct as he shook hands with Piers, his smile a little apologetic. April guessed there was no real malice in him.

But like many of the ton's young bucks, he had too big an allowance and too much time on his hands. She guessed he enjoyed it, too.

"Have you met my wife?" Piers was asking, and April approached, offering her hand.

Darcy took it, bowing over it with some grace and style. As his gaze lifted to hers with what she guessed was practiced flirtation, it clung, and his eyes widened to something like wonder. No doubt that was practiced, too.

"Lady Petteril," he breathed, then cleared his throat. "Your servant, my lady. How delightful to meet you at last. I have only ever admired you from a distance before."

Was he actually blushing? Could one practice that too? "We're very glad to see you. Are you acquainted with our cousin, Miss Withan? And Sir Peter Haggard?"

Darcy bowed to them, too, then followed her to the sofa, sitting beside her as she poured him a cup of tea. At least he said nothing about poor Bernie. Yet.

Haggs set down his cup in its saucer and rose to his feet. "Since I can interest no one else in the expedition, I shall take myself for a lonely drive around the park. Miss Gussie." He bowed perfunctorily. "Withy, don't decamp without a word. No need to ring, I can see myself out. Thank you for the tea and the company, Lady Petteril." He kissed her hand, in clear contrast to his cool leave-taking of Gussie, nodded to Darcy, and sauntered out.

Gussie glanced up toward the closed door, and just for an instant, her expression was one of *anguish*. What the devil was going on between that pair? Gussie caught April's eye and hastily looked back toward the window.

"Hope you don't mind my interrupting," Darcy said. "Wanted a particular word with you, Petteril."

Gussie rose. "Would you please excuse me? I feel a bit of a headache coming on."

Darcy stood politely as she flitted across the room.

"Lie down," April advised, frowning with genuine worry, though she suspected the girl chiefly needed a few minutes alone to cry. "I'll come up shortly."

Piers addressed their remaining visitor with his usual focus. "Is it about the baby? Or the hackney?"

Or Bernie?

"Both," Darcy said. He looked content enough as Piers sat back down, clearly not intending to whisk him away to a male only study. "For one thing, I saw that hackney again."

He glanced from Piers to April and seemed to rear into the back of his chair, perhaps disconcerted by the intensity of their joint focus. "That is, I don't *know* that it was the same one, but it was driving very slowly around the square. It did that twice while I walked from my front door, and then it passed me going into Park Lane at a fast trot. There was no one inside it, so he hadn't picked anyone up."

"When was this?" Piers asked.

"Before midday, about half past eleven or so I suppose. I was on my way to the club."

"Was it the same driver as last time?" April asked, frustrated because if it was Tucker, they had missed him simply by looking for him. Was there some connection between Tucker and Essie Brown?

"I couldn't say. I didn't get a good look at him before. But I made sure to remark everything I could about him this time, all right and tight. Youngish fellow, hat pulled quite low over his forehead. Brown coat. With a small flower in his buttonhole. His horse was a dappled grey."

"That's *him*!" April exclaimed, meeting her husband's gaze. "Could he have been looking for us while we looked for him?"

Piers frowned. "Maybe. Or he was sent by Essie. Or was looking for..." He tailed off, before he said the Parks' name. "At any rate, it's dashed odd behaviour."

"Maddening," April agreed.

Darcy, who had had been glancing from one to the other as they spoke, now said with some fascination. "You are looking *together* for this fellow?"

"It's become a bit of a habit," Piers said at his most vague, which meant he was thinking.

Darcy set down his cup and saucer on the table in front of him and shifted position again as though uncomfortable. "There's more. About the baby."

They both regarded him expectantly. He cast a glance at Piers that was almost pleading, then shook his head.

"Not a good man, Lady Petteril. No point pretending I am. Thing is, when I heard about the baby, it bothered me. Because I thought I'd dreamed of one, on steps that might have been like those down to your kitchen area. And I began to wonder if it *wasn't* a dream. I even began to wonder if I'd thought it funny to wander off with some poor woman's child and dump it at your door. No idea why I would do such a thing, but there it is. A man in his cups doesn't always make much sense, and I confess I was deep cut, utterly mauled if you want the truth."

"Did you?" Piers asked steadily.

Darcy blinked, as though dragging himself back to the point. "Did I take someone's baby? No, thank God. But I've been remembering as my mind cleared, and I *did* see it on your steps when I was on my way home. I don't know why, but I was holding on to your railings—having a rest, I expect—and I saw something move just toward the bottom of the steps. Rags in a box shifting about on their own. Just the thing to fascinate a man drunk as David's sow. So down I went, poked the rags, and there was this little baby, sound asleep. Had the tiniest little ears, ridiculously small and yet perfectly formed. So, I covered them up again to keep him warm."

"What did you do then?" April asked with some fascination.

"Well, it struck me whoever had put the baby there might come out of the house and find me where I'd no business to be. Which seemed terribly funny at the time, so I chortled my way back up the steps and weaved my way across the square to my own place." He scowled. "Which was when the horse and carriage knocked me down."

"Hadn't you noticed the hackney before that?" Piers asked.

"Can't say I did. Not at my best, old boy."

"No, I can see that." Piers was frowning. Like April, he was clearly wondering how this fitted into the overall story, if they had learned anything new for it.

The most interesting point, April felt, was that Tucker had come back today, had been watching and waiting. For what? One of the Parks? For Mrs. Robb to appear with the baby? For Piers?

Or for Darcy...?

She sat bolt upright. "Mr. Darcy, did you *see* someone put the baby on our step that morning?"

Darcy rubbed at his forehead. "If I did, I don't recall it."

"You think Tucker knew he'd been seen and tried to run over the witness?" said Piers, who had never been slow.

"It crossed my mind. Perhaps he came back today, looking for Mr. Darcy, but didn't see him in time. He galloped past, but of course, Mr. Darcy was sober and he didn't wobble into the horse's path. And there would have been too many people around for him to drive straight at him." Too many people, including Bernie the stable boy whom they could have put in danger...

Piers gazed at her, considering as he always did. He rubbed his chin with one finger. "Possible. But..."

"Speculation," she said with a sigh.

"Melodrama," Piers corrected. "Which doesn't necessarily rule it out."

"Have a scone, Mr. Darcy," April said, offering him the plate.

ON HIS WAY BACK TO the house, after spotting Darcy mount the Petteril House steps, Bernie skidded into the stables to see how many horses, grooms or coachmen lurked there. This was the quickest way of finding out if his lordship was at home or if Bernie needed to warn Mr. Park about the Darcy cove. Bernie didn't think her ladyship should see Darcy without protection.

All the horses were there, and something moved in the far corner, where the hay was piled.

"Mr. Johns?" Bernie called to his immediate superior, peering, for the back of the stables was dim and gloomy.

There was no answer. All was still, and yet Bernie knew someone was there. The hair on the back of his neck stood up.

He didn't like being afraid, so he glared at the hay pile. "Look, I ain't got time for this. You want me to bring all the men out to find you, that's fine with me. We'll see which of us gets in trouble for that!"

"Don't," the hay pile whispered. "Please don't. I'm just resting and don't mean no harm."

"Come out then," Bernie commanded.

There was a distinct pause before the hay rustled and a pair of ancient boots topped by a skirt and apron appeared from behind the pile. She moved slowly, stiffly, as if it was painful. But eventually, the cloaked, huddled figure of a young woman was complete before him. A girl, really.

"What are you doing in here?" he asked severely.

The girl glanced fearfully toward the open door.

"You're hiding," Bernie guessed.

"Don't tell, please don't tell. It's only for another hour till I'm sure he's gone and then I'll get off. You'll never know I'm here."

Bernie was a soft-hearted lad underneath his bluster, and he was not immune to female helplessness. The girl was skinny and poor and was clearly frightened to death.

"If the others find you, I can't help you," he muttered.

"They went up to the house."

"They'll be back." He took a step nearer as she wobbled and swayed. "Here, are you hungry?"

"Thirsty," the girl whispered.

Bernie gave her the flask Lord Petteril had given him in case he was kept out all day. He had been disappointed to discover it was only water and not ale.

She drank as if she was desperate, then quickly handed it back. "Thank you."

"You'd better hide right at the back of the hay," Bernie said. "No one's likely to come that far back, even for the evening feed."

"Oh, I'll be gone long before then."

"Where will you go? Home?"

She shook her head.

Bernie remembered well enough the terror of having nowhere to go. In his case, he was lucky, and his uncle had got him the job here. This girl didn't look as if anyone was caring for her.

"Stay in here for tonight," he said impulsively. "It's warm enough with a couple of blankets. I'll bring you one and there's others spares in here though they stink of horse. You'll need to stay quiet, mind 'cause Mr. and Mrs. Johns lives above, and so do me and the grooms. I'll get you some food, too, though it won't be much."

"You're kind," the girl said. "Thanks." She backed away, toward the hay. "Is... Do you work for Lord Petteril?"

"I do," Bernie said proudly.

"Has...have they got a baby in the house?"

Chapter Eleven

Leaving Piers to see Darcy out, April hurried upstairs to see Gussie. In fact, her greater urge was to go to the baby and make sure he was still happy without Mrs. Robb's provisions, but she forced herself to go to Gussie first.

The girl was not lying in bed in a darkened room with a cold compress on her head, as April half-expected. Instead, she sat in the chair by the hearth, gazing into the flames. Which might have been why her eyes were red, though April doubted it.

Gussie made an effort, smiling at her. "Has your admirer gone?"

April blinked. "Mr. Darcy? He just had something to get off his chest." She sat in the chair on the side of the hearth. "I think you should follow his example. What has made you so dislike Sir Peter?"

One hand lifted and fell helplessly back into her lap. "Of course I don't dislike him," she said in despair. "But he wasn't meant to come here, not yet!"

"Why not?" April asked, none the wiser.

"Because...*this*!" She held up both hands, pointing all her fingers toward her face. "I look terrible!"

April's lips twitched, which was an entirely unhelpful response, and besides, it wasn't truly funny. Fortunately, Gussie did not notice.

"You have been very ill," April said. "And it's true you're still a little pale and thin, but *terrible*? Hardly. Sir Peter will just be glad to see your health improving. Which it won't, Gussie, if you keep getting so overwrought about nothing."

Gussie pushed her head back against the chair. "I know, but I can't help it. I wanted to take him by surprise in the spring with my brilliant beauty. Pathetic, isn't it?"

"No," April said carefully. "But, if this means you have a decided preference for Sir Peter, what on earth makes you believe he is so shallow?"

"Shallow? Of course he is not."

"Would you dislike him if he started looking a bit peaky?"

"Of course not," Gussie said impatiently. "But men are different. They care about how females look. What do you imagine all the primping and fashionable gowns of the Season are all about? Attracting the right male attention. And don't look at me like that! If you imagine Piers would have married you if you hadn't been beautiful as well as clever—"

"I never thought I was beautiful," April blurted. Though Piers had told her so, she was merely glad of his bias and kindness. It had never been about beauty…had it?

"Well, you are," Gussie muttered.

Brushing this aside, April tried a different tack. "Is Sir Peter handsome?"

Gussie blinked. "I don't know. I like the way he looks."

"I expect he likes the way you look too. But if he likes you, Gussie, he likes *you*. If he's worth anything—and I believe he is—he would never be put off by a little thinness of the face. What might put him off is rudeness."

Gussie closed her eyes. "Was I awful? I had a plan, you see, and he ruined it by turning up."

April leaned forward. "You really *weren't* pleased to see him, were you?"

Gussie shook her head. "But April, I miss him now he's gone. Am I very foolish?"

"Yes," April said, smiling. "But the position is not irretrievable. We'll see him again before we leave. And you must concentrate on rest and recovery. Now, would you like to go for a drive or have you exhausted yourself?"

IN FACT, GUSSIE FELL asleep still curled in the chair, so April covered her with a blanket and left her to it.

As soon as she stepped into the passage, she could hear the baby crying. She bolted along the passage to her dressing room.

There she discovered Janey had taken over Martha's baby-watching duties. The girl stood over the baby's cradle, her hands over her cheeks in helpless despair, while Georgie bawled his little eyes out.

"Oh my lady, I don't know what to do with him!" she cried. "I've changed his nappy and given him a cuddle, but every time I lay him down, he cries and won't stop till I pick him up again. And Mrs. Robb said not to pick him up all the time."

Well, Mrs. Robb is not here. April picked the baby out of his box and his wailing cut off like a tap. The little lips stretched and his watery eyes positively sparkled.

"He smiled at me," April gasped, and her heart broke into a thousand pieces.

PIERS SAT IN HIS FAVOURITE armchair in the library, his legs stretched out in front of the fire and crossed at the ankles. It was a good position in which to think, and his mind was certainly rushing.

Baby Georgie. *This* house. Tucker and his hackney. Darcy. Essie Brown. Mrs. Robb kept popping in there, too, as did the Parks to whom he and April owed so much. The trouble was, he couldn't fit them into a pattern that made sense, even leaving half of them out. Too many characters or too few?

He couldn't tell because they were desperately short of evidence to prove anything at all beyond the existence of a baby discovered the morning before last.

Georgie, this house, Tucker...

The library door burst open and April flew in.

Blinking himself back to reality, he acknowledged the baby in her arms and the fact that her lovely face was wreathed in smiles. His heart turned over, for she was happy. Blazingly, deliriously happy.

"Piers, he smiled at me!"

His heart contracted and he found himself standing up to look. Georgie kicked one leg and fixed imperiously onto Piers's eyes with his own.

"He's not smiling at me."

April brought up her little finger and tickled the baby's cheek. He kicked both legs and turned his face into April's breast, burrowing.

"He's hungry," April said uneasily, "and Mrs. Robb isn't back yet." She touched the corner of Georgie's mouth, and he latched his lips onto her finger.

Piers laughed. "Well, that seems to be fooling him for a bit."

Not for long, however. The finger quickly proved unsatisfactory, and he let it go to do some glaring and more quick, heavy breathing instead.

April rocked him in her arms in a panicked sort of a way. "Oh dear. I'll ask Mrs. Park. Maybe he can take a bit of water or something?"

While Piers moved toward the bell rope, April was already halfway to the door. She clearly meant to go in person to the housekeeper. As worried for her as for the baby, Piers gave up on the bell and merely accompanied her to the kitchen.

This fresh appearance of their lord and lady in the servants' domain, bearing the baby did not cause consternation so much as chaos. Busy maidservants bearing glasses and piles of linen, swerved to get a closer look at Georgie, thereby getting in the way of a footman carrying a heavy tray, who was paying more attention to the newcomers than to where he was going. Bernie the stable boy, clutching a plate of Mrs. Gale's special door-stop sandwiches for growing boys, gawped at his godlike employers with child and almost fell over a pail of water Janey had set down to scrub the kitchen table. The water slopped over the side of the bucket, and Mrs. Gale tutted in disapproval as she sailed past it toward her visitors.

As queen of her domain, Mrs. Gale welcomed the viscount and viscountess without looking at them, all her softened focus on the baby in April's arms, who was now whinging, though whether at the noise in the kitchen or the fact that April had been forced to stand still, was not clear.

"He's hungry," Mrs. Gale observed.

Bernie glanced at his sandwiches and looked guilty.

"I know," April said. "I was hoping Mrs. Robb had stopped for a cup of tea down here."

"No, she's not back yet. He must be due for a big spurt of growing, the greedy little fellow. Here, Janey, is there any water left in that kettle? Pour a little bit into a bowl and bring it over. Sit down here, my lady..."

Under everyone's gaze, Piers and April sat at the kitchen table with the baby. Janey brought a bowl of water from the kettle, which Mrs. Gale tested with the tip of her finger. "Stick your finger in the water, my lady, and see what you can dribble into his little mouth while he sucks it."

To Piers's relief, this seemed to work, for the wailing and fussing stopped. Whenever Georgie released April's finger, she hastily dunked it into the water again and thrust it back into his eager mouth. It was peculiarly fascinating. Even more so was the soft expression on April's face. He could almost have believed the child was hers, and that caused a tumult in his heart, shot through with pain at her inevitable grief. And his own.

He spared a glance around his gathered, gawking household—which now included Park himself. Bernie, at least, gave the impression of trying to tear himself away, backing toward the kitchen door with his sandwiches untouched.

Mrs. Park emerged from her sitting room, as though roused by the sheer inactivity of the kitchen. "Why are you all standing around here? What on earth...?" She broke off in astonishment as she caught Piers's gaze. "I see. Well, it doesn't take all of you supervising! Let's have the lamps lit. Janey, get that table scrubbed and the bucket out of the way. Francis, Martha, to the dining room with you. Are you still here, Bernie?"

Reluctantly, everyone began to move again, when a loud knock sounded on the area door. Bernie froze again. Everyone looked to Park for guidance—presumably since the ejection of Essie Brown.

Park squared his shoulders with a certain grimness and sailed across the kitchen to answer the knock himself. Piers rose, directing Francis with his eyes. The footman set down his tray and moved to stand in front of April and the baby, while Piers followed Park to the area door, watching from the kitchen doorway as the butler turned the key in the lock.

Park opened the door and froze, staring at whoever or whatever stood there. Piers clenched his fists.

"Evening, Dad," the visitor said.

PIERS CAUGHT HIS BREATH, tensing as the unseen male voice spoke. Park slowly stepped back from the door to make way for the newcomer.

A familiar sense of helplessness washed over Piers. Whoever stepped inside his house, he would not know them, would have no idea what danger they truly represented. Outside, dusk was falling and the shadow from the recently lit kitchen lamp fell across the man who entered Petteril House.

He was about Park's own height and removed a hat that had seen better days. He carried no weapon. Park closed the door behind him and gestured toward the kitchen. The visitor obeyed in equal silence, though he was brought up short by Piers, who did not retreat from the doorway.

In the lamplight, he could see now that the visitor was young, about the same age as Piers. Or Tucker, perhaps. And like the hackney driver, he was dressed for warmth rather than respectability. There was no flower in his buttonhole. And no immediate threat in his face. *Had he seen it before?* Damn it, there was nothing he recognized.

"My lord," Park said in a strange, hollow voice that set all Piers's nerves on edge. "This is my son, Simon."

Which was the one thing Piers had already grasped.

Simon gave a slightly jerky bow.

Uneasy, Piers thought, *and slightly thrown*, which might have been good. Certainly, the man made no effort to bolt or attack, so taking his cue from Park, Piers inclined his head and backed into the kitchen to make way.

Mrs. Park had clearly rushed across the kitchen for she stood only feet away from Piers now, perfectly still, her avid gaze drinking in the figure of her son. Simon made an instinctive move toward her, and halted himself at once, but as though his action had broken a spell, Mrs. Park hurled herself over the distance and seized him in her arms.

Simon hugged her tight, his face anguished, his eyes closed. Piers relaxed just a little, and risked a glance at April, who still sat where he had left her, her little finger in the restive baby's mouth. A faint twitch of her shoulders told him she knew no more than he. But then, she had never met Tucker.

Mrs. Park drew herself free of her son and, suddenly brisk, dragged him by the hand past Piers and toward the kitchen table, where she pointed to Georgie.

"Is this yours?" she asked harshly.

As Piers silently crossed the floor to observe better, Simon raised his hand to rub the back of his neck, as though trying to work out what she meant.

"Is what mine?" he demanded at last.

"The child!" exclaimed his mother.

Simon's eyes widened. "Don't be ridiculous. I've never met the lady in my life!"

Piers choked back an impossible breath of laughter. April's eyes began to dance.

Simon's mother clouted him across the shoulder. "This is Lady Petteril!"

Simon blushed to the roots of his hair, a hunted look flooding his face, though he managed another of his jerky bows. "Sorry, m'lady," he mumbled.

"Is this your son?" Park asked clearly.

"No, of course not!" Simon said. "What *is* this?"

Piers decided it was time to intervene. "I would suggest that we retire to your sitting room, Mrs. Park." He cast a quick glance around the kitchen, using the same expression as he had once employed around his Oxford office and lecture halls. He was gratified to see it worked just as well on servants as on distracted students. They immediately plunged into motion. Francis retrieved his tray, following Martha and her linen to the stairs. Bernie and his sandwiches sloped off to the back door. Janey began to scrub the kitchen table with a hard brush.

Piers, April, and the baby followed all three Parks into the housekeeper's sitting room. At the last moment, Piers swiped up the bowl of water that was keeping Georgie quiet.

Simon glanced around his mother's private domain with apparent approval, while Mrs. Park settled April and the baby in her usual chair. Piers set down the bowl on the little table on their far side, and perched on the arm of his wife's chair, leaving the other for Mrs. Park—who, however, seemed too agitated to sit in it.

Park said harshly, "You will answer all of Lord Petteril's questions with honesty. If you're still—" He caught his wife's eye and subsided, but the damage was done.

"If I'm still capable of honesty?" Simon said bitterly. "Don't you know?"

"Enough, Simon," Mrs. Park said quietly. "We need the truth now. All of it. How long have you been…" She swallowed. "How long have you been free?"

"A few weeks."

"Have you seen That Woman?"

Simon's shoulder twitched with irritation and pain. "Once. She still won't leave him, so I came south alone. I thought his lordship was asking the questions?"

"Do you have work in London?" Piers asked.

"Temporary, gardening in the parks which is really just tidying up at this time of year. But it keeps me in the open and I like that. They might keep me on in the spring. And I see you sometimes, walking past." His quick glance took in both his parents, and Piers, touched, warmed to him a little.

"I never saw you," Mrs. Park said hoarsely. "You never spoke."

This time, Simon's glance was at his father. "Wasn't sure of my welcome, was I?"

Piers shifted against the chair arm to make more room for April. "So why now?"

Simon met his gaze without fear. "Because a Lord Petteril asked for me by name at my lodgings and gave this address. I knew my parents worked for you, because my mother wrote and told me when I was still in prison. What I didn't know was why you were looking for me. I didn't want you dismissing them because of their association with me, so I stayed out of the way. Then I wondered if that would have the opposite effect, so I thought a discreet call on my way home from work might be the answer. It seemed to be when my father opened the door, though then I seemed to walk into a circus. Or a mad house."

April laughed and stood up. "Come, my lord. I think it's time we left these people to a more private reunion."

Piers, both glad for the Parks' sakes and frustrated by the dissolving of all his suspects, rose with alacrity.

April paused and glanced at Simon. "Mr. and Mrs. Park are welcome to receive visitors at their own discretion," she said and led the way out.

Piers was proud of her.

As soon as he re-entered the kitchen, he saw a female-shaped silhouette hurry past the window that looked onto the area.

"It's Mrs. Robb!" Janey called.

And just for an instant, April looked stricken.

"I'M GLAD SIMON ISN'T Tucker," April said as they changed for dinner that evening. "I like him."

Which was also in his favour, Piers allowed.

"Though now we're running short of suspects," she added. "Even if it was this Tucker who left the baby, why did he pick our step in particular?"

"Perhaps he didn't. Perhaps it was just chance." Piers set about fastening the tiny loops of her gown. He would miss this intimacy if she ever found a lady's maid. "I just can't understand why he would come back in the middle of the night. In any case, the hackney that Darcy and the servants saw is not necessarily Tucker's."

"We still need to speak to him."

"We do." Piers dropped a kiss on her tempting nape and stood back to let her fasten his sleeve buttons, which he was quite capable of doing himself. But he enjoyed inhaling the light, floral scent of her skin and watching her face as she concentrated on this small, wifely duty. "And I think Darcy's honesty clears him too."

"Even if he did see anything else useful at the time," April said, switching to the other sleeve, "I doubt he'll remember it now."

Piers regarded her quite carefully. "He is not completely harmless, you know. You will please be careful around him."

She glanced up at him in surprise. "Why?"

"April, he is smitten, and to a rake all women are fair game."

"Even married women?"

"*Especially* married women."

She searched his eyes for a moment, a smile beginning to dawn in her own. "Are you jealous, Piers?"

She seemed more delighted than annoyed, forcing him to smile back. "I am careful of my wife—who might not realize that drawing room wiles and tavern attacks have different approaches. Though they amount to the same thing."

She stood on tiptoe to kiss his lips. "I'll be careful."

"Good." He reached for his coat and shrugged into it.

April went to the bed to pick up the shawl she had left there. "Piers?"

"Yes?"

"If we can't find Georgie's parents...we could keep him, could we not?"

The moment was here, sooner than he'd expected. He hated that she was afraid to face him while she asked. He moved to stand behind her and placed his hands lightly on her shoulders.

"I can't give you children," she blurted. "But we could have *him* as our own."

"It wouldn't be fair, April," he said gently. "He can't be my heir and whether we have children or not, he *would* be treated differently from our own—passed over as my heir to lands and title, resented by servants, looked down on by people we might regard as his peers though no one else would."

She half-turned to face him. "Like me?"

The cut sliced through him. "Yes," he said brutally. "Like you, but worse because he didn't choose it and wouldn't understand it."

"But we can't give him up to the orphanage!"

"No, we can't do that either. We will think about it if we can't find his parents, but I haven't given up yet. Have you?"

She butted him, burying her face in his shoulder. "No," she whispered.

Chapter Twelve

Although April's breath at his neck was even and soothing, Piers could not sleep. He worried about her and distracted himself by worrying instead about the baby and his failure to find out the truth about him. Although he truly hadn't given up, he did recognize that the chances of success were low. So, he thought about April again and the circle of anxiety continued throughout the night, through short dreams and long spells of wakefulness.

April had fallen asleep as soon as her head touched the pillow, as though exhausted by sheer emotion. He could not bring himself to wake her, but he slid from the bed and crept into his dressing room. Five minutes later, he was walking downstairs by the light of a solitary candle.

Only Janey was in the kitchen. "Morning, my lord. The kettle's just boiling if you want coffee."

"Thank you," he said and watched her pour a few previously ground beans into a cup and cover them with hot water from the stove. He left it for a bit, then picked up the cup with a nod and wandered toward the back door. "Best lock it behind me."

He sat on the garden bench, listening to the first wakeful chirps of the birds and watching the dawn break. He could almost imagine himself in the country, except for the distant sounds from other kitchens and the nearby roads where horses and vehicles and pedestrians were already moving.

He thought about saddling his own horse, then decided to wait for the grooms to get up, which they would do soon enough now. Reaching the sludge at the bottom of his cup, he abandoned it and ambled across the garden to the mews. He walked from one end to the other, thinking about Simon and his prison sentence for striking a man who beat his wife. He thought of the hackney that had all but run Darcy over after Darcy had seen Georgie on the area steps of Petteril House. He thought about April and her instinctive love of that abandoned baby. And his own instinct to protect them both.

Grooms were stumbling out of the mews buildings, including his own men who all shambled up the garden path to the kitchen, including Bernie. He still needed to ask Bernie where Darcy had gone yesterday, though his urgency about the matter had quite faded.

Wandering past the gate, he thought he could smell Mrs. Gale's first breakfast serving of porridge and milk, ham and eggs, and lots of tea.

Was Tucker the hackney driver at his breakfast already? Did his wife rise and prepare it for him? Or did he buy it from a stall like Jack Newly's on the way?

Reaching the end of the mews, Piers discovered he was cold without his overcoat. Time to go back and wake April and break his own fast. Or should he go alone to find Tucker?

Bernie slipped out of the gate clutching a large, heaped plate, taking it furtively back to the stable as though to protect it. Where did the boy put all that food? He wasn't feeding bacon to the horses, was he?

Piers smiled to himself. In retrospect, Ape had never been that ravenous. Not after he had begun to live here. Had any of the others seen the clues that Ape was not a growing young boy but a fully adult if undernourished woman?

And he was back to unease over April's unhappiness, and the baby. *Think of Tucker and flowers and well-baked pies, and frightened flower girls* - anything that would not paralyze him into blackness.

Abruptly, he halted. His hand was already on the gate, but he didn't open it, for *now* his mind was racing, lining up the truths and questioning them until, surely, the only possibility was left.

He had to know.

Turning, he actually ran the length of the mews in the direction of the park and emerged into the street to see Jack Newly the baker setting up his stall alone in the wintry half-light. A lantern hung on the side of his stall. There was no sign of the flower girl, although her empty barrow stood again beside the railings.

Newly must have heard his running footsteps, for he half-turned, an expression of surprise on his face. "Where's the fire, sir?" he asked lightly.

"Good question," Piers replied, slowing to catch his breath. "Here's another: what's the flower girl's name?"

Even in the odd light, he saw the shutters come down in Newly's eyes. His smile was fixed. "Ginny? She's a good girl, sir, hard-working and respectable, always—"

"I have no designs on her virtue," Piers interrupted. "Her surname?"

A frown creased Newly's brow, as though he couldn't find a reason for the question. Or a reason not to answer. "Tucker."

Tucker.

Part of Piers sagged, though not really in relief. He was right but the tragedy remained.

"Where is she?" he asked steadily.

"Flower market, probably. She'll be along later."

"Like yesterday? Hidden behind you and Reg the Veg in case she sells anything?"

Newly took the bait, his eyes spitting. "It's not like that at all!" He broke off, biting his lips and closed the lid of his stall with distinct clatter.

"No, I don't really believe it is," Piers admitted. "But you are hiding her, aren't you? She's frightened and probably hurt. We had our eye on you, in case you were bullying her, squeezing her out, but it was never you. You were just hiding her from Tucker. He beats her, doesn't he?"

"Since they were married," Newly said, rage in his voice. "Bastard! What man of any feeling, any honour, could lay a finger on that girl? Her own husband who's meant to protect her—knocks her around like a football, though never her face, only places she can cover up—and she does. She took it for more than a year, defending him when I saw the bruises on her arm, when she could barely walk for the pain. Still, she took it all and stood up for him until he..."

He swung away again, swiping a pie from his stall and handing it to a man in a cloth cap Piers hadn't even seen approach. The exchange was quick and mechanical, pie for coin, with a couple of nods and barely a break in stride for the customer.

"Until," Piers said, "Tucker discovered he could hurt her more through the baby." He had heard about the healing bruise on Georgie's arm, which had supposedly been struck against the side of his box, a difficult feat... "Ginny Tucker brought the baby here with her, didn't she? The morning we found him on the doorstep."

"He drives a hackney," Newly said. "He used to work afternoons and late evenings, so when she was selling her flowers, he was at home with the child. But she got too afraid to leave him, so she brought him here with her."

"But he knew where to find her," Piers said. "She caught sight of him the other morning and bolted, left the child on my doorstep to hide him. Tucker followed her in his hackney and lost sight of her. I doubt he'd have seen the baby, even from his box, because whether from luck or cleverness, she had placed him so close to the wall. He hung around the square waiting for Ginny to come out of her hiding place—which I suspect was the narrow passage along the side of my house. From there, she probably fled via the back garden.

"The funny thing is, my neighbour rolled home and *did* see the baby before we did—largely because he was holding himself up by holding on to my railings. Maybe Tucker thought he lived there. In any case,

Tucker gave up and drove around the square, probably with ever increasing anger until he almost ran my poor neighbour over.

"Which," Piers finished, refocusing his attention on Newly, "explains why there was no sign of the flower seller when I rode past to the park a few minutes later. When I rode home, she was back at her barrow. I should have seen how upset she was."

"She knew the child was in your house," Newly said. "She thought you were kind and he'd be safe with you and your lady wife."

"Did she go home?" Piers asked, his mouth dry with fear.

Newly shook his head. "I looked after her barrow at night and she stayed with a friend. Tucker found out, of course, fortunately not when Ginny was there, and the friend asked her to leave. You're not meant to come between a husband and his wife, are you? It's the law that she and that child belong to Tucker, even though he'll kill them in the end. I'd kill him myself only then who'd look after Ginny?"

He looked up and down the street, served a couple of customers, then, as if he'd made up his mind, he swung back on Piers.

"I've lost her," he blurted. "I don't know where she is. Me and Reg, we helped keep an eye out for Tucker, kept her hidden from him as best we could, found a place she could slip through the railings and hide. He came by in his hackney yesterday, before midday, and she bolted. And never came back. I can't find a trace of her."

He stared at Piers, his face anguished with raw emotion. "What if he's killed her?"

It was terribly, tragically, possible. But as the last suspicion slid into place, Piers doubted it. And crossed his fingers.

"I don't think he has." Piers nodded curtly and walked away back toward home. The wind was icy.

Behind him a shout went up from Newly. "Reg! Reg! Hurry up! Mind my stall for a few minutes!" Then came pounding footsteps, and Newly was striding along beside him.

"Is she with you?" he burst out.

"Oh, not with me," Piers said vaguely. "If I'm right, then she's safe. But for God's sake, keep your eyes open for Tucker. One more question, Newly. He must have known you were hiding her. He must have worked out she bolted at first sign of his hackney. But all he needed to do was leave it around the corner, walk a few yards and grab her. He had every right to take his wife home. No one would have stopped him. The law is all on his side. Why didn't he?"

"Because law or no law," Newly said savagely, "he knows I'd kill him."

<hr />

APRIL WOKE WITH THE knowledge he was not beside her and sat bolt upright in bed. Her head reeled with the speed of her movement. So did her stomach.

He was rising too early again. She had been vaguely aware of him tossing and turning in the night. She had been so proud that since September, when their true marriage had really begun, he had been sleeping soundly and contentedly. Puzzles worried at his mind of course, and this one was special for many reasons, but his wakefulness made her uneasy. Especially if it had more to do with her. With her talk of keeping the baby, with the reminder of her own barrenness.

No one is happy forever. Who had said that to her? It didn't matter. It was true that no one could ever be happy every minute of every day. She did not expect Piers to be. But it was the depth of his unhappiness she needed to watch and manage. The very idea of him slipping back into what he called the blackness, terrified her.

She slid out of bed, washed and dressed hastily in yesterday's morning gown—and missed Piers's helping her with the ridiculously tiny hooks. A shawl covered her failure to fasten most of them and she sallied forth in search of her husband.

Her stomach rumbled. And toast, perhaps. Or at least a biscuit...

The kitchen was the first room she had ever seen in Petteril House. Admittedly she hadn't seen much of it then, since she'd only had a dim lantern and pots and pans had been of little interest to a thief in search of a jewel safe. But it had been her first home too, or at least the first she could really remember, and she was quite comfortable marching down there in search of her husband the viscount.

Rather to her surprise, she found him immediately, pushing Jack Newly the pie man into a chair at the table while Mrs. Gale poured him a cup of tea.

The pie man?

Piers glanced up and their eyes met.

No blackness, only blazing determination that took her breath away.

"You've solved it," she blurted.

"I worked it out," he said, like a correction, "with the aid of Mr. Newly here. Come out in the garden and I'll tell you."

With a bewildered nod to Newly, who had jumped to his feet at first sight of her, she snatched a piece of toast off the plate on the table and followed Piers to the back door.

In the garden, they sat on the bench, shivering in the cold, while he told her what had suddenly become clear to him in this very spot only half an hour or so ago.

"I think it was the similarity in the stories that led me there," he said. "Simon going to prison for defending the woman he loved from her abusive husband. And your telling me that Ginny the flower seller was frightened. My thoughts about the mystery and you had become so muddled I knew you must have told me something important. Between us, we must have *seen* something important. I wasn't paying much attention at the time, but the morning we found the baby and I bought you flowers, Ginny had white Christmas roses in her barrow."

"And her being Tucker's errant wife explained him hanging around the square—even his trying to break in here the other night. He must have been looking for his wife as well as the baby. Because you'd told him along with the others at the hackney stance, exactly where the baby was."

Her toast suddenly tasted like ashes and she lowered it, staring at him in sudden fear. "Oh, Piers, he moved house suddenly the day after, saying his wife had gone earlier. What if he found her and hurt her so badly that she... We haven't seen her for days. What if she's dead?"

"Well, I don't think she is," Piers said, standing up. "Let's go and see."

He offered her his arm and she was glad to accept it, abandoning the remains of her toast for the birds. But he didn't go back to the house. Instead, he turned toward the garden gate out to the mews.

The groom lounging in the stable doorway, sprang to attention. "'Morning, my lord. My lady."

"Is Bernie inside?" Piers asked casually.

The groom opened his mouth to bellow a summons, but Piers forestalled him, saying hastily, "We'll go and speak to him there."

"Is he in trouble?" the groom demanded.

"Oh, no."

Bernie was right at the back of the stable, carefully grooming one of the carriage horses. He dropped the brush, possibly by accident, though he rushed forward to meet them. "M'lord, m'lady, I followed the cove just like you said but he didn't do nothing but go to his club and his friends paid me to follow him too. I kept the money though I'll give it back if you want me to. And then he just came back here but Mr. Park knew all about it."

"I know," Piers said gravely. "You did very well. Thank you." He held out the promised coin but held onto it when the boy grasped it. "You had better tell Mrs. Tucker to come out. She is quite safe."

Bernie gawped. April suspected she did the same.

It took a moment, but the hay pile rustled and then slowly, uncertainly, her gaze darting all around, Ginny the flower girl emerged.

Tears were streaming down her face. "Oh, sir, oh ma'am, oh *please* keep my baby safe..."

"You're both safe," April said, going to her because she could do nothing else. "We'll look after you now."

"I didn't mean to do the wrong thing, sir," Bernie was saying anxiously to Piers. "She were just starving and needed a place to hide and I didn't miss one of my sandwiches..."

"I'd say you should have told me," Piers said, "but then I neglected to ask you about yesterday at all."

Ginny Tucker was thin and frail, and her whole body was heaving with grief and fear and probably physical pain. Her story was not new or unusual. April had even guessed at it—without the connection to Georgie.

Georgie...

How blind I have been...

"Come," April said gently, although her arms already ached. "I'll take you to him. He's missed you."

MRS. PARK WAS NOT GETTING much peace in her private sitting room. When April had closed the door on the mother and child whom she left in there, the first person she saw was Mrs. Robb, sitting at the kitchen table beside Jack Newly. Despite the company, the nurse looked curiously alone. Her expression was numb.

Without meaning to, April put a hand on her shoulder. No words were necessary or wanted. In fact, April didn't even want to think.

She gazed at Piers, who sat, frowning, astride one of the kitchen chairs.

"It's a mess," she said frankly. "Ginny can't go back to him, and we have no right to keep them from him. Wherever we send them, he'll find them, because all the places we have are yours and therefore easy to find."

"It's Tucker who needs to be sent away," Newly said savagely. "Preferably for life."

"You're not to touch him," April said severely.

"Agreed," Piers said, lifting his chin from his hands. "But Newly is right."

April glared. "Only the law won't touch a man for beating his wife or his child."

"It will, however, punish him for other crimes."

Newly cocked a hopeful eyebrow in his direction. "Has he committed any?"

"Not yet," said Piers, rising to his feet.

"Oh no," April said.

"I'm your man," Newly said, his eyes gleaming as he stood beside Piers.

"Sadly, you can't be," Piers said. "There must be no contact between you and Tucker now. But don't worry. There will be plenty of witnesses. I even know a Bow Street Runner."

Chapter Thirteen

Amos Tucker was not a man much given to remorse. As his parents had taught him, and his life to date had confirmed, he was always right. If he lost his temper—as he frequently did with his silly, maudlin little wife who was trying to turn his fine son into a soft mama's boy—then the fault lay with whoever had caused his anger. He went to church. He was a good man. Everyone told him so, and he tended to agree that he had done nothing in his life to reproach himself with. He had always obeyed the laws of God and man.

On the other hand, he did tend toward the belief that it had been a mistake to break into Lord Petteril's house. Not that the pampered lord didn't deserve it for keeping Tucker's wife and child from him, but the act did actually put him in the wrong. Moreover, if he had been caught, as he so nearly was...

He still shuddered at the memory, for his throat still hurt. He hadn't thought his face was visible in the darkness during that brief struggle, but Petteril still suspected him. He had been to the hackney stand looking for him, and had even gone to the old house, according to his neighbour. Thank God he'd told no one the address of his new lodgings.

On the other hand, he hadn't worked all day either. And while frightening his errant wife into another bolt might have been amusing, even satisfying in its way, it had not ultimately been successful. He would try again later today, whenever a fare took him in that direction.

He pulled his horse up behind the last hackney in the Oxford Street queue and saluted with his whip a couple of the fellows gossiping at the side. It behoved him to keep a weather eye out for Petteril, of course, but he expected him to have given up. As he would, sooner or later, give Ginny up too.

He contemplated with some pleasure how he would make Ginny suffer for her fall from grace—for the sake of her own soul, naturally. And just as naturally, Tucker would forgive her and take her back. After which, the mighty Lord Petteril would owe him some compensation. After all, the man had a new wife, had he not? So what the devil he was about, installing Ginny and the brat in his own house, Tucker had no idea. The man was blatant and ungodly and should pay...

Dear God was that him?

The viscount strolled into his line of vision from behind, a rather lovely lady on his arm who was most certainly not Ginny. This girl, though probably about the same age as Ginny, was vital and brilliant and wore beautiful clothes.

Hastily, Tucker pulled his muffler up and his hat down, but too late, the aristocratic eyes swept over his person, freezing his blood. The funny thing was, Petteril showed no sign of recognition but sauntered on toward the gossips.

Unable to quite believe his luck, Tucker urged his horse to walk forward the few feet necessary to close the gap that had opened in front.

Perhaps Petteril was not looking for him. After all, it would have been a miracle if he'd made out Tucker's face in those few moments of struggle. His lordship had no real reason to believe Tucker was involved. He must just have been asking around about him and no doubt the other jarveys too.

All the same, Tucker would be happier when he had a fare.

Too late, he remembered that Brearly, one of the jarveys Petteril was talking to, had been there on the previous occasion too. Would it matter? Brearly was grinning, and nodding, damn him, right at Tucker. The fool even raised his hand.

Tucker wondered if he should bolt again and had to remind himself that he was not in the wrong. Lord Petteril had stolen his wife and child, and Tucker was quite sure he wouldn't want the beauty on his arm to be aware of that.

Lord Petteril sauntered up to him. "Mr. Tucker," he said affably. "I believe I have something of yours."

Well! That was blatancy with a vengeance. Tucker had to close his lips tight, for he did not want the world to know his wife had run away to this fop with his ridiculous quizzing glasses—two, no less!—dangling around his neck. One of them came into play as the viscount appeared to inspect Tucker's coat.

"No buttonhole today? I suppose there can't be Christmas roses at your new home."

"Can I help you guv'nor?" Tucker said aggressively. "You want a hackney, you got to take the one at the front."

"Oh, no, I just wanted a chat. Would you care to come down to save the crick in my neck?"

"I would not," Tucker retorted, his eyes flickering to the young lady who had separated herself from Petteril to stroke the horse's nose. "Mind out, missus, he don't like strangers and he's quick to bite."

The girl glanced up at him boldly, amusement in every line of her face. "What, *this* well-mannered gentleman?" The treacherous horse snuffled and ducked his head nearer her. "Nonsense."

God, she needed schooling. Raising her eyes, disputing a man's word and judgement... She must be the viscountess, he supposed, but that was no excuse. He felt like jerking on the reins to make the horse walk over her feet.

"Yes, I have your buttonhole," Lord Petteril said unexpectedly and with perfect clarity. "You left it behind when you tried to break into my house the night before last."

"Here, you can't go around saying things like that!" Tucker said furiously, for the viscount's voice had carried and an audience was gathering. "Brearly, fetch the Watch, this gent's mad as a sack of frogs."

Before his eyes, the affable and empty-headed fop turned into a haughty, hard-eyed aristo. "I don't like your tone fellow."

"You's the one who spoke to *me*, guv'nor," Tucker said triumphantly. "I'm just doing my job!" He was about to tickle the horse's ear with his whip to instruct him to once more close the gap in the queue of carriages, but the beast was already walking to the urging of the girl who was leading him as though he was her pet dog.

Tucker's whip hand itched.

"That's true," Petteril allowed. "I did speak to you first. Thought you'd like to know how your son is."

"My son?" The words spilled out before he could think.

"Her ladyship and I are—er... looking after him for you, at the request of your wife."

"She got no call to do that—and no right neither. You give me back my son—and send that good-for-nothing woman with him."

"So you can hurt them again?" Petteril asked.

Tucker wanted to smack that smooth, supercilious face. Except, to his annoyance, the listening crowd looked shocked, and he felt compelled to win them back and turn them against the ungodly dandy trying to torment him.

"A woman needs discipline. So does a son."

That made the fool speechless! Not so the wife, however, who said in disbelief, "*Discipline?* At six weeks old? Or less?"

A rumble of shock swelled in the still growing crowd. More well-to-do people had stopped to join the throng listening in to this confrontation. How had it even got this far? It was a nightmare he wasn't sure how to end.

"You do know infanticide is a crime?" Lord Petteril said conversationally.

"I never killed no infants, least of all my own," Tucker said furiously. "You got no call to say such lies! There's laws against that too!"

"Lies?" Petteril looked baffled.

"I never killed my son!"

An "Ooh" rumbled around him, and it was not friendly, for he had spoken too loudly. Tucker's whole body heated with embarrassment and outrage at the injustice—why did people assume his denial was an admission of guilt? He blamed the whole thing squarely on the manipulation of the swaggering nob before him. Tucker needed to get away from here before the crowd turned nasty.

"So you just *disciplined* your son?" Petteril said. "What did he do? Break wind? Steal your gin? Talk back to you?"

"I don't drink!" Tucker roared, though that was not strictly true either. "You give me back my stolen child!"

"Come and get him," Petteril invited, bowing and gesturing gracefully that he should come down.

Which gave Tucker all the excuse he needed to escape. The crowd would think he was driving away to retrieve his son, and he would be out of this nightmare—at least in the short term, which was all he really cared about right now.

But the wretched woman stood in front of the horse, holding its head and the red mists of fury began to descend on Tucker. She was in his way. Before he could even think what he was doing, he lashed out with his whip, straight for her pretty, pampered face.

It should have hit her, too, laid open her skin, only she had reflexes like a boxer. She jerked aside, freeing his way.

He yelled, "Yah!" and lashed with the reins instead. But quite suddenly, the fop below launched himself from the ground and landed with a bump beside him on the box. Somehow the whip was ripped from his hand, and he stared into black, fathomless eyes that promised him death.

In sudden blind fear, he struck out, and his fist connected with flesh and bone.

IN HIS UNIVERSITY CAREER, Piers had once been quite adept at gaining and retaining the attention of unruly, generally arrogant young men, though he could not recall ever using ridicule before. But he saw at once that like the students, Tucker was over-conscious of the opinion of others.

Even so, riling and ridiculing did not appear to be sparking the kind of attack he needed Tucker to make against him. At this rate, the man was simply going to escape him, and then it would all be to do again.

Until Tucker lashed his whip at April. And then there had been no thought in his head, no planning, only blind instinct and fear for her. He might even have yelled out some bizarre war cry as he leapt for the box of the moving hackney and wrenched the whip from Tucker's hand.

Too late to prevent the lash, but the bastard would never make another. And he knew it. He saw it in the man's suddenly terrified eyes.

"Piers!"

The cry penetrated the fury of his brain but before he could respond, something struck him in the mouth. And the shoulder and the face.

"Piers, he missed me!"

Of course he did. April had spent most of her life dodging blows. She had the reflexes of a cat.

And Tucker had hit him.

They had won.

In fact, Tucker was still hitting him, though they were too close together for the blows to have much weight. It was more like panicked scrabbling, or the sort of childhood fights he had had with his brother and cousins.

The fear and fury that had impelled him up here vanished into something very close to laughter. As he fended off the blows, trying to still and capture Tucker's wild hands, he became aware of the surging crowd he had deliberately attracted. All the jarveys were there. Vehicles had stopped in the road as men abandoned their horses and ran across to either help or watch the fun.

Tucker was trying with all his body weight to shove Piers off the box. It was instinct to push back, which Piers did, pushing the man hard against the back of the bench. He was almost in control when the horse, either frightened by the crowd or inadvertently instructed by the ribbons tangling between himself and Tucker, took off.

The hackney veered around the vehicle in front and galloped wildly up Oxford Street. Piers released his man to seize the ribbons instead, and Tucker, with a yell of fear, hurled himself inexplicably toward the road.

Piers made a grab for him and caught a handful of coat in one hand.

Someone screamed. A horse neighed and stamped with clear anxiety. Several people bolted out of the way of the hackney. Piers managed to haul the dead weight of Tucker upright onto the box.

"Woah, there, horse, gently, my friend," Piers soothed and quickly brought the horse back to a standstill at the side of the road. After all, it hadn't really had time to get the bit very firmly between its teeth for a decent bolt.

Everyone was rushing toward them, a sea of people with indistinguishable faces. Piers turned his head and looked at Tucker.

Terror still stood out in his eyes. And that, Piers felt, was well-deserved.

PIERS FELT SLIGHTLY numb as they finally walked toward home. There had been enough witnesses to the whole scene—including their friendly Bow Street Runner, Jimmy Knott, who just happened to have been passing—to tell the full story of the confrontation. Tucker had attacked Lady Petteril with his whip, Lord Petteril had defended her, and Tucker had then attacked him, after which the horse had bolted and Tucker had inexplicably tried to jump into the road. Fear again.

No one would have been to blame for the injury or death of Tucker except Tucker himself.

Only that wasn't strictly true.

Piers had set out to provoke an assault. He couldn't even say he had not intended the man to die, because there had been a moment, when Tucker had wielded that whip...

No one would hurt April again while Piers lived. And certainly not with impunity.

"It didn't go quite according to plan," she said.

"No," Piers agreed.

"Why did he try to jump?"

"Fear," Piers said. "And panic. It ruled him, I think. That's why he needed to make his wife afraid of him."

She thought about that for a bit. "What will happen to him now?"

"Transportation, probably. Ginny and Georgie will be free of him, at any rate."

She squeezed his arm. "Then we did what we set out to do."

Jack Newly was at his stall, gazing at them. Piers lifted one hand his thumb pointing upward and Newly grinned hugely.

"He'll help look after them now," April said. "Piers?"

"Yes?"

"Why did you save him?"

"Instinct." But he would remember the earlier impulse, too, the one that had terrified Tucker in the first place.

She brushed her cheek against his shoulder. "You are the best of men."

He wished that was true.

BY AGREEMENT, APRIL wrote a glowing reference for Mrs. Robb—or at least Piers wrote it and April signed it. She had been practising her signature and it now looked quite ladylike. They gave the character to her with a packet containing rather more than her fee.

"A present for your daughter," April told her. "Rent a better place to stay. Between the agency and the recommendation of my husband's connections, you will do better. Later, you might consider housekeeping as an alternative."

Mrs. Robb swallowed audibly, but seemed to have no words beyond a hoarse, "Thank you. My lady. My lord. May I say goodbye to Georgie?"

They must all say goodbye to Georgie. Piers's heart contracted, though April merely said breezily, "Of course!"

Though his name was not really Georgie but Amos, like his father. Piers was glad his mother called him Mo.

April went shopping with Gussie. And when they came home, she busied herself with packing for Haybury Court. She did not go near the kitchen, where little Mo was ensconced in his new cradle with his loving mother and the devotion of the servants. She was brittle, avoiding the pain of the parting.

And yet she did go down to the kitchen to be with him when Jack Newly came to collect Ginny and Mo. Her eyes stayed dry and she kept smiling. And Piers's ache was nearly all for her.

※

THE FIRST THING HE noticed, entering his bedchamber to change for dinner, was the absence of April. Her brushes and the perfume bottles he had given her had vanished, presumably back to her own room.

It was a good thing to be back to normal, he assured himself. He just needed to give her time and space to grieve. And pray it did not take her away from him.

So, he changed into evening dress, dragged the comb through his hair, and strolled through to April's rooms, which were no longer locked to protect the privacy of Mrs. Robb.

She was sitting at her dressing table, staring into the glass so hard, she didn't even notice him until he stood behind her and she saw his reflection.

She smiled at once, a forced smile that meant nothing. Except pain.

"Don't pretend, April," he said. "Not with me."

She blinked at the glass, then turned to face him. "I'm not pretending. I just want it to go away."

"You want what to go away? Pain?"

She nodded. "It will pass. He was never ours."

He took his courage in both hands, because there had always been truth between them. "But the pain was there before you got fond of Georgie. Before he even landed on our doorstep, you were losing your...sunniness."

"I didn't mean to," she whispered, staring at him, her eyes full. "I just... I want things I can't have. I'm all jumbled inside, and it frightens me."

"You are unhappy."

"Sometimes. At others, most of the time, I'm very happy until something makes me sad or angry or..." She trailed off, searching his eyes and must have found the truth there for she suddenly jumped to her feet, seizing him by both shoulders.

"No," she said fiercely, "no! Without you, I would *die*..."

He held her, burying his lips in her hair. "Then what is it?"

"I don't know," she mumbled into his coat. "I can't think. Everything is new and I don't know where I am. Sometimes I think I'm drowning... I don't feel like *me* anymore."

"You're still you," he said huskily. "And you're still wonderful. I think we need to go home."

Her fingers tightened, digging into him. "We do. I believe we do. And everything will be better."

"Can you last another two days?"

"With you," she whispered. "With you."

Chapter Fourteen

The odd conversation with Piers made April feel better. She wasn't sure why, since she hadn't really been able to tell him much and he certainly had no solution. But she was touched that he had seen, that he cared.

Between that evening and leaving for Haybury Court, her time was eaten up with preparations for the journey and farewells to their few friends in London. Haggs had called to say goodbye and Gussie had behaved much more civilly to him.

And they spoke to the Parks about the possibility of Simon taking on the position of head gardener at Haybury Court when the current, rather ancient incumbent, was induced to retire.

They were to spend one night at Maria's, and then they would be home. Which left just the hurdle of someone else's baby to admire. And the dowager, of course, who, during Maria's recovery, was acting as hostess.

Lady Petteril swept them all upstairs almost immediately to admire her grandson. They were met at the door by the proud father, Sir Jeremy, who shook Piers's hand as if he was somehow responsible for this new happiness.

Maria looked well and contented, although she voiced her determination to rise for dinner. Her baby, even tinier than Georgie, looked like a helpless little prune, and yet, inevitably, emotion surged in April so that she could do nothing but smile in silence.

Maria, something of an unknown quantity to April, smiled back at her. "It will be your turn soon."

She couldn't have known how much that hurt.

April was glad to be shooed out of the room and taken to her own, which she fully expected to be on the other side of the house from everyone else's. But the manor house was not so huge, and, in fact, she was given the chamber next to Piers. Her bags had already been unpacked and her things put away.

"This is lovely," April said, more for something to say. She couldn't understand why the dowager was still in the room with her.

In fact, the older woman was scowling at her, as she often did, her nostrils flaring.

"You're looking peaky, April," she said abruptly. "Are you quite well?"

Hoping her jaw had not dropped in astonishment—not least because the dowager had used her Christian name—April replied, "Of course. I'm just tired from the journey."

"You've been tired for a bit."

And Lady Petteril had noticed?

"Are you *enceinte*, April?"

April's stomach tightened. It was a pain she must learn to deal with.

"I mean increasing," the dowager said, flushing slightly. "Expecting a baby."

"Yes, I know what it means," April replied, "but no, I'm afraid not."

"Are you sure?"

Too sure.

"When did you last have your courses?"

April couldn't remember, except it hadn't been since Christmas. In fact, it had been at Haybury Court, well before they had leapt to Aunt Prudence's summons. Early December? Which was...

"It's the second of February," Lady Petteril said matter-of-factly.

April stared at her. "But I can't be!"

"Well, I don't believe he's never touched you," she retorted, holding up one hand with her fingers splayed so that she could count them off.

"No bleeding. You're more tired than usual. I expect you're over emotional too?"

"Well, yes, actually...."

"And you *feel* different?"

The blood sang in April's ears. "I do," she whispered.

With unexpected gentleness, the dowager pushed her into the nearest chair before her knees gave way. Lady Petteril said something else, something to do with the viscount's heir, but April wasn't listening.

She was drowning in the relief of understanding, and in the intense wave of happiness sweeping up from her toes. Energy sparked, igniting a flame of excitement, and she sprang to her feet.

"Piers!" she shouted at the top of her voice, flying across the room, only to bump into her alarmed husband at the door. "Oh Piers, you'll never guess!"

Lady Petteril sniffed. "He won't."

But he was soon informed, at which point the dowager, revolted by such a vulgar display of affection, was forced to leave the room.

Lord Petteril Mysteries (so far!)
Petteril's Thief
Petteril's Corpse
Petteril's Ladybird
Petteril's Portrait
Petteril's Wife
Petteril's Folly
Petteril's Christmas
Petteril's Baby

About the Author

Mary Lancaster is a USA Today bestselling author of award winning historical romance and historical fiction. She lives in Scotland with her husband, one of three grown-up kids, and a small dog with a big personality.

Her first literary love was historical fiction, a genre which she relishes mixing up with romance and adventure in her own writing. Several of her novels feature actual historical characters as diverse as Hungarian revolutionaries, medieval English outlaws, and a family of eternally rebellious royal Scots. To say nothing of Vlad the Impaler.

More recently, she has enjoyed writing light, fun Regency romances, with occasional forays into the Victorian era. With its slight change of emphasis, *Petteril's Thief*, was her first Regency-set historical mystery.

CONNECT WITH MARY ON-line – she loves to hear from readers:

Email Mary: Mary@MaryLancaster.com
Website: http://www.MaryLancaster.com
Newsletter sign-up: https://marylancaster.com/newsletter/
Facebook: https://www.facebook.com/mary.lancaster.1656
Facebook Author Page: https://www.facebook.com/MaryLancasterNovelist/
Bookbub: https://www.bookbub.com/profile/mary-lancaster
X: @MaryLancNovels https://x.com/MaryLancNovels
Bluesky: @MaryLancaster.bsky.social
TikTok: https://www.tiktok.com/@mary.lancaster1

Printed in Dunstable, United Kingdom